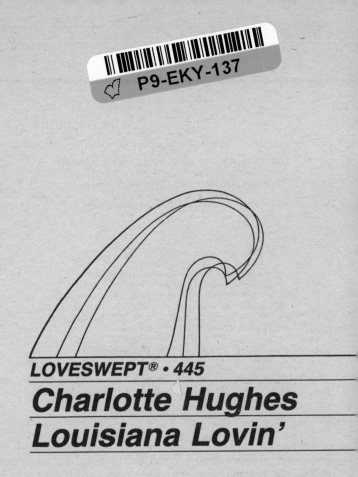

LOVESWEPT® • 445

Charlotte Hughes
Louisiana Lovin'

BANTAM BOOKS

NEW YORK • TORONTO • LONDON • SYDNEY • AUCKLAND

LOUISIANA LOVIN'

A Bantam Book / January 1991

LOVESWEPT® and the wave device are registered
trademarks of Bantam Books, a division of
Bantam Doubleday Dell Publishing Group, Inc.
Registered in U.S. Patent
and Trademark Office and elsewhere.

If you would be interested in receiving protective vinyl
covers for your Loveswept books, please write to this
address for information:

Loveswept
Bantam Books
P. O. Box 985
Hicksville, NY 11802

ISBN 0-553-44085-3

Published simultaneously in the United States and Canada

Bantam Books are published by Bantam Books, a division
of Bantam Doubleday Dell Publishing Group, Inc. Its trademark, consisting of the words "Bantam Books" and the
portrayal of a rooster, is Registered in U.S. Patent and
Trademark Office and in other countries. Marca Regis-
trada. Bantam Books, 666 Fifth Avenue, New York, New
York 10103.

PRINTED IN THE UNITED STATES OF AMERICA

OPM   0 9 8 7 6 5 4 3 2 1

"We need to get out of these wet things," **Michelle said.**

She saw that Gator was literally soaked to the skin. His denims were plastered against his thighs and calves in a way that made her mouth dry. His shirt was drenched as well, and hung open to his waist, exposing his wide chest where black hair glistened wetly. She blushed profusely when she caught Gator staring at her in her soaked white nurse's uniform. He still had the power to make her body go berserk.

"That's the best idea I've heard all day," Gator said, shrugging out of his shirt. Michelle wondered if he had any idea how sensual the simple act was. In movement, he was rippling muscles and taut flesh. Michelle had seen enough male bodies in her job to know that his was one of the best she'd ever laid eyes on.

"Like what you see, Mic?"

Her face flamed. "I was just . . ."

"Staring?" He looked amused.

"You haven't changed at all, Gator—you're still impossible."

"You've still got the prettiest green eyes I've ever seen. Not to mention the cutest rear end. You've improved with age." He stepped closer. "So, you're a nurse now. Remember when I suggested we play doctor so you could practice on me?"

"I said no. I knew what ailed you, and I wanted no part of it."

"One kiss for old times' sake, Mic. I was your first, wasn't I?"

"Not the first to kiss, nor the last, Gator," she said quickly.

"But I bet I'm the one you remembered best." He stepped closer and his mouth captured her in a sudden, warm embrace. . . .

WHAT ARE *LOVESWEPT* ROMANCES?

They are stories of true romance and touching emotion. We believe those two very important ingredients are constants in our highly sensual and very believable stories in the *LOVESWEPT* line. Our goal is to give you, the reader, stories of consistently high quality that may sometimes make you laugh, sometimes make you cry, but are always fresh and creative and contain many delightful surprises within their pages.

Most romance fans read an enormous number of books. Those they truly love, they keep. Others may be traded with friends and soon forgotten. We hope that each *LOVESWEPT* romance will be a treasure—a "keeper." We will always try to publish

LOVE STORIES YOU'LL NEVER FORGET
BY AUTHORS YOU'LL ALWAYS REMEMBER

The Editors

Dedication: To my sons, Patrick and Eric,
for all the sleepless nights you gave me
as babies, and all those left ahead.
I love you.
Mom.

*   *   *

My sincere thanks to Mike Adams and Kathy Shortridge, captain and first mate of the MAJIC charter yacht out of Venice, Louisiana, who personally took me through the bayous and taught me how to eat crawfish and cherry bombs. And to Ralph Garrison, owner of the BLUE GOOSE, who showed me how to enjoy simple pleasures. And to the wonderful people of Tickfall for making me feel so welcome.

And a special thanks to my husband, Ken, who does all my proofreading for me. Thanks, honey.

One

The rain fell in earnest now, pelting the lush vegetation along the grassy banks of Lizard Bayou. A bullfrog belched in protest as a strong gust of wind shook the tall reeds and Virginia creeper at the riverbank. Fan-shaped palmetto leaves bowed low in the breeze as a carpet of duckweed was swept to one side of the bayou, where it nestled among knobby cypress knees and flowering water hyacinths. Overhead, the August sky hung like a giant water-filled canopy about to burst. A blast of wind sent water spraying through an open window, and Michelle Thurston slammed it closed.

She tossed her grandmother an angry look. "Reba Kenner, you are the most stubborn, hardheaded, obstinate old fool I ever laid eyes on. You're a dead woman, you know that? If you stay here, you're as good as dead."

The elderly woman obliged her granddaughter with a smile and a nod. At eighty, Reba Kenner was a shrunken version of her former self. But her skin was smooth and unmottled and her nappy white hair clean and healthy looking, the result of a concoction she'd drank for years that she declared was two parts bayou water. It was the same remedy she'd insisted her granddaughter drink as a teenager to ward off acne and was the reason, or so Reba said, that at thirty, Michelle's complexion was as flawless as a baby's, and her long strawberry blond hair thick and beautiful. But if Michelle looked anxious, her grandmother was anything but. "Would you like more coffee now, dear?" she asked at last in a pleasant, fruity-textured voice.

Michelle fixed her green-eyed gaze on her grandmother, her anxiety and frustration mounting, much as the wind outside had in the past hour. "Have you even heard a word I've said, Grand?" she demanded.

"I heard most of it," the woman confessed, "but I may as well tell you the battery went dead on my hearing aid day before yesterday, and I haven't replaced it. I thought maybe we'd go into town while you're here."

Michelle stared at the woman in disbelief. "Grand, we can't go to town. We're under a hurricane warning."

"They're calling it Katie, you know."

"That's right. And it wiped out part of Cuba last night. Do you understand? It's probably going to wipe us out too." Michelle resisted the urge to shake her grandmother as she spoke—*anything* to make her see reason. She was exhausted after having pulled the graveyard shift in the emergency room the night before, during which time she'd made periodic checks on the storm's progress. Since her parents were out of the country on business, it was up to her to see about her grandmother. Then, at five A.M., the storm had changed its course, and it had become obvious that Louisiana would get hit. Because Reba had no use for telephones, Michelle had had no way of calling her. She'd made the two-hour drive from Baton Rouge in record time, arriving in Lizard Thicket shortly after nine that morning, still wearing her nurse's uniform. Now, she was tempted to throw the slight woman over her back and run for her car before their time ran out.

Reba continued to stroke the gold tabby cat in her lap, and the cat purred loudly and curled into a fat ball. "I'm not leaving my animals, Mic," she said, her eyes suddenly bright with tears.

Michelle had only seen her grandmother cry once, and that had been at her grandfather's funeral. To her, the scene was as traumatic as those she faced in the emergency room, and she felt her own eyes sting at the sight. She glanced around helplessly at the menagerie of animals. At least a half-dozen cats lay sprawled on the furniture and the old-fashioned braided rug in front of the fireplace. In the kitchen, a blue-tick hound named Mae West had recently given birth to eight puppies. A large antique birdcage in the dining room held a large green parrot named Mister Ed, who hadn't stopped squawking since Michelle arrived. "I suppose we could take them to Baton Rouge with us," she said doubtfully, swallowing the lump in her throat. She almost shuddered at the thought of all those animals riding in her brand-new Mustang convertible. And to think, she'd paid extra for those white leather seats.

Reba chuckled. "I can just see all that fur a-flyin' now. That hound won't let anybody or anything within six feet of those puppies."

Michelle sighed heavily and sank onto an old wicker rocker that matched nothing else in the room. Reba's house had always looked as though it had been furnished from a neighborhood garage sale. She threw nothing away. Everything in the house was either patched or mended, and even Michelle, who preferred newer styles, had to admit the furniture was very comfortable. What she'd give to curl up and take a nap on her grand-mother's vintage iron bed.

"I should have known you'd fight me over this," Michelle said tiredly. "What am I going to do with you, Grand? You refuse to put in a telephone, and you never answer my letters. You're becoming more of a recluse every time I see you. How is anybody supposed to know if you're sick or injured, for Pete's sake?"

Reba reached over and patted her granddaughter's hand affectionately. "I can take care of myself, dear, really I can. And you know how much I like my privacy." She clucked her tongue. "You're just tired. You always did turn into a fussy little thing when you were tired. Why don't you lie down on the sofa and rest. This old house is a lot stronger than you think. Why, I've ridden out more storms in this place than I can remember. And so have you, if you'll think back over the summers you spent here as a child. We'll be safe."

Michelle knew it was useless to argue. When Reba made up her mind, no one could change it. She could beg and plead till doomsday, and it would only fuel Reba's determination to stay. "I suppose we should get the house ready," Michelle said at last, pulling herself up from the rocker. She didn't know where to begin. She was trained to handle emergencies—it was what she did best. But most folks cooperated in tense situations, and Reba was doing her best not to.

Michelle tried to think of everything they might need if the storm hit hard—and she had no doubt it would. It had slammed into Cuba during the night, packing 110-mile-per-hour winds, leaving thousands homeless. And just when everybody thought it would go back out into the Gulf and die, it merely picked itself up and turned due north. It was scheduled to hit Pensacola, Biloxi, and New Orleans that afternoon.

And then she heard it. At first Michelle thought it was the wind, but the grinding noise persisted. She hurried over to the window, wiped the steamy glass with the ball of her hand, and peered out. A small motorboat, barely visible in the rain, rounded the bend of cypress trees. "Somebody's coming," she said.

"In this weather?" Reba pushed herself up from the chair and joined her granddaughter at the window. "Oh, that'd be Gator Landry," she said, taking one look at the small skiff. "He's our new sheriff. 'Course, Gator ain't his real name. He was named Matthieu after his daddy. But folks 'round here have always called him Gator. I don't reckon I know why."

Michelle's eyes widened to the size of half-dollars. "Not the Gator Landry I met the summer I turned fifteen?" she asked in disbelief, remembering the wild, black-haired, black-eyed Cajun who'd teased and tormented and pursued her unmercifully that year. "Somebody actually made him sheriff?"

Reba chuckled. "Aw, Gator's okay," she said. "I reckon he's got a wild hair in him, but if he turns out half as well as his daddy, he'll be a good man. His daddy was sheriff for almost thirty years, you know." Reba paused. " 'Course Gator wasn't none too pleased when the folks here elected him. He put up quite a stink. He'd made a little money on a sugar cane plantation south of here and had his heart set on taking it easy for a while. Yes, it really riled him when they made him sheriff."

Michelle pressed her lips into a grim line. "Why'd he take the job?"

Reba shrugged. "Aw, this town's been good to Gator's family. Their house burned to the ground when he was just a young'un, and the folks here got together and built them a fine new place. Gator's mother still lives there, and while he was gone all those years making his fortune, the folks here took care of her. Besides, our last sheriff wasn't worth a cuss. He'd just sit back and let that wild bunch from the pool hall terrorize the old folks 'round here. I s'pect he was scared of 'em. Anyway, the town booted him out and 'lected Gator sheriff. Everybody knows that Gator Landry ain't scared of nothin' or nobody." She chuckled.

"He raised holy hell, though, when he found out they'd made him sheriff without his permission." Reba's smile drooped, and her look turned serious. "Then somebody went and attacked Gator's own mother and stole her purse. She wasn't hurt none, but it made Gator see red. First thing he did was close down the pool hall."

Michelle shook her head. Gator Landry was one of the last people she'd have expected to run into after all these years. Of course, it was bound to happen sooner or later in a place the size of Lizard Thicket, where almost everybody was related by blood or marriage. "Why do you suppose he's here?" Michelle asked, watching the man in a bright yellow slicker dock his boat beside the small pier at the back of the house. Rain sluiced down his head and shoulders and broad back. He was an imposing figure, even at a distance.

Reba pressed her lips together in annoyance. "I'm sure he's going to try and make me leave," she said. "But I ain't going." Reba threw open the back door and leaned out. "Git in this house, Gator," she yelled, trying to make herself heard above the wind and rain. "You gonna drown out there in that weather."

For a moment, the only sound Michelle heard other than the wind was her own heartbeat. She chided herself for the attack of nerves. Heavens, she and Gator had been children that summer, no more than fifteen years old. Knowing Gator, he probably wouldn't remember her, she told herself.

There was the sound of footsteps on the back porch, and a moment later, Gator Landry stepped through the doorway, a hulking figure with sweeping shoulders, dripping water onto Reba's plank floor. He wrenched off his hat, and he winced as though the effort had cost him dearly. His eyes were bloodshot, his face had a pea-green cast, and Michelle thought he looked as though he could be sick with very little trouble.

"Reba, I guess you heard the storm turned on us," he said, his deep voice, seasoned with an accent that was uniquely Cajun, reverberating off the walls of the house. He shook his head, and tiny droplets of water flew in every direction. "I have to get you out of here. We're setting up shelters in town now."

"I'm not going, Gator," Reba said, hitching her chin up stubbornly. "You know they won't let me bring my animals into those shelters, and I refuse to walk off and leave them defenseless. Besides, my granddaughter will take care of me."

Gator shot her a questioning look, then glanced around the room before his gaze collided with Michelle's. For a moment, they merely stared at each other, and the silence in the room was as deafening as the wind and rain outside. "What are you doing here?" he asked, his tone almost accusing.

His abrupt manner surprised her. So he did remember her, Michelle told herself, giving none of her own thoughts away in her cool appraisal. She let her gaze travel the length of him. He was still about as rugged as they came, she decided. Too rough around the edges to be classically handsome, but striking enough to turn any woman's head. His nose and mouth were a bit pronounced, an indication of his heritage, but while those same features might appear unsightly on another man's face, they added character to his. And, Lord, she hadn't forgotten those onyx eyes. That hooded gaze could penetrate a stone wall and turn a woman's knees to gelatin at the same time. He'd filled out and grown taller. He was at least six feet six. The khaki-colored shirt he wore strained against a massive chest, upon which a gold sheriff's badge had been pinned. His legs were encased in a pair of denims that molded to him like a leather glove, and the holster he wore held a flashlight, a nightstick, and a revolver. He was certainly different from the men she worked with, who wore neat slacks and crisp white lab coats.

Michelle was able to speak at last. "Hello, Gator," she said. "I thought my grandmother might need me . . . what with the storm coming and all."

"You shouldn't be here. Neither of you. This storm is right on our tails now. I've got to get you to safety."

"I'm not going anywhere," Reba said, and Gator and Michelle glanced up quickly, as though they'd forgotten she was in the room. "Besides, I ain't scared of no storm," Reba added, crossing her wiry arms over her bosom.

Gator sighed heavily and raked his fingers through his blue-black hair. Damn, but his head hurt. He probably had the worst hangover of his life. This storm was the last thing he needed. "Now, Reba, don't put up a stink over this," he said. "When this hurricane hits it's going to rip this place apart, and you won't be able to help yourself, much less those animals. Come get in the boat before it fills up with water and sinks."

"I ain't goin', Gator, and that's final." Reba marched over to a chair and sat down stiffly. Her look was unyielding. "I reckon at my age I should know my own mind."

"Then I'm going to pick you up and haul you out to the boat," he said, his look as deadly as the approaching storm. Reba gripped the arms of the chair.

"And I'll kick and scream this house down over our heads," she said.

"Oh yeah?" Gator planted his hands on his hips and glared at the woman. "Then I reckon I'll have to shoot you."

"Leave her alone," Michelle said.

One pair of black eyes snapped up in surprise as Michelle closed the distance between herself and the sheriff. "You can't force my grandmother to go with you. And all the threats in the world aren't going to make her change her mind."

Gator suddenly looked amused. She hadn't lost her spunk, thank goodness. He rocked back and forth on the heels of his boots. "Aw, Reba knows I won't really shoot her. I may just have to rough her up a bit."

"Now, children," Reba admonished gently. "Let's don't fuss. We're just tense because of the storm." She pulled herself out of the chair. "Come on in the kitchen, Gator, and let me give you something to eat. You look awful. You must've had a late night."

"Now, don't go trying to change the subject on me, Reba." He followed her into the next room.

"But I will take a glass of tomato juice if you have it. And a couple of aspirin," he added hopefully.

Michelle stood there dumbfounded. She followed them and watched from the kitchen door as Gator accepted the aspirin and washed it down with a tall glass of tomato juice.

"I don't believe this," she said. "You have a hangover. And you call yourself the sheriff? Why, your eyeballs look like they're about to bleed, and you look as though you just crawled out of bed. And is that a hickey on your neck, for heaven's sake?"

Gator set his empty glass on the kitchen table and faced the younger woman. "Look, lady," he said, planting his hands firmly on his hips. "It's nobody's business how I spend my Saturday nights. I give these people twenty-four hours a day, six days a week, and if I want to have a little fun come Saturday night, that's my affair. I got a half-dozen deputies who can take over in my absence. Now, could we stop harping on my personal life and get out of here? I don't have all day."

When Reba spoke, she was adamant. "This is the last time I'm going to tell you, Gator: I ain't going. Stop pestering me."

"I oughtta lock you up and throw away the key, Reba Kenner," he said. He regarded the older woman for a moment. "If you won't think about yourself, think about your granddaughter. Are you willing to put her life in danger too?"

Reba was clearly shaken at the thought. "Then make her go with you, Gator. But I can't leave.

I'd never forgive myself if something happened to my animals."

"Don't be ridiculous, Grand," Michelle said. "I'm not leaving you." Michelle walked over to her grandmother and took one spindly hand in her own. "We'll be okay," she said to Gator, sounding a lot braver than she felt. "You'd better go before the weather gets worse," she added after a moment. For some reason, she was in a hurry to see him go. Seeing him again after all these years had shaken her more than she dared admit, taking her down memory lane to a simpler time filled with sweet anticipation. He appeared just as wild and reckless as he'd always been. But then some things never changed, she told herself. Gator would always remain just beyond a woman's grasp. Capturing him would be like trying to catch a puff of smoke and hold it down.

Gator looked from one woman to the other. It was obvious Reba's granddaughter was trying to get rid of him. Impatience and anxiety were written all over her pretty face and magnified in those emerald-green eyes. Lord, those eyes! He could see forever when he looked into them. And that yellow hair. It had just enough red in it to appear fiery. He could still remember how silky it felt against his bare chest. Aw, damn, he thought. That was the last thing he needed to think about.

Gator shoved his thoughts aside. He had to concentrate on protecting them. He was the sheriff, it was his duty. It didn't matter at the moment that he didn't want the job, had *never* wanted the job, for that matter. Until he found somebody capable of taking his place, it was his responsibility. "You're both crazy, you know that? If something happened to either of you, it could be days before someone found you."

"Why are you telling me this?" Michelle asked, growing irritated at his insistence. Why wouldn't the man just go, for heaven's sake!

"Because it's up to you to convince your grandmother to leave," he said.

"And I've been trying to do just that for the past hour," she said. "Do you expect me to just drag her out by her hair?"

He muttered a curse that brought a rosy blush to the older woman's face. "Reba, have you got any plywood lying around?" he asked at last.

The abrupt change of subject surprised both women. "I reckon there's some under the house," she said. "Why?"

"I'm going to have to board up these windows," he said, motioning to the large plate-glass windows that dominated the back of the house. Although the house opened onto a screened porch, he knew a strong wind could shatter the glass or toss something right through it. "Nothing like waiting till the storm is right on your butt to start taking precautions," he muttered, pulling on the hood to his slicker. He glanced at Michelle. "See if you can find me a hammer and nails."

"You're not staying," Michelle said hopefully.

"I'm sure as hell not leaving the two of you out here alone," he said, already heading toward the back door. He slammed out of it a moment later.

The women stared at each other in disbelief. Michelle shook her head, a feeling of dread washing over her. "Better tell me where the hammer is," she said. "I don't think we're going to get rid of him." She didn't know which she dreaded most—the storm, or spending time with Gator Landry.

Gator found the plywood stacked neatly under the back of the house. He muttered another string of curses when he realized he'd have to crawl under the place to reach it. He rolled his eyes heavenward. Why had he let them pin that badge to him in the first place, he asked himself for the umpteenth time. He'd had it made in the shade at the time—money in the bank, a decent place to live, and enough willing women to warm his bed at night.

Gator dropped to his belly and shimmied beneath the house toward the stack of plywood. Hadn't he paid his dues with hard work? Lord, he'd sweated in those sugar cane fields for ten years before he'd made the place profitable. He'd done without material things and gone hungry at times, just to put every dime back into the crop. And it had paid off. He'd figured on retiring for a couple of years—sleeping late, fishing from his houseboat, taking his time before he found another good investment. And then a bunch of old fools had gone and elected him sheriff. Worse than that, they'd made him feel obligated, as if he *owed* them! That's what really irked him most, he decided. He didn't owe these people anything, and if they expected him to attend some damn law enforcement classes for six weeks just so he could do a job he hadn't wanted in the first place, they could think again. He'd show 'em the error of their ways. Of course, he would keep the job until he found out who'd messed with his mother. He couldn't wait to get his hands on the vermin responsible for that. Once he took care of that little problem, he'd resign and be done with it.

But first he had to get through this emergency, Gator reminded himself. No matter what, he had to take care of Reba and that granddaughter of hers who thought herself too good for the likes of him, had *always* thought herself too good. Boy, what he'd give to take that woman down a notch or two and prove that she wasn't the Queen of Sheba. It might do her some good. He wondered for a moment if she was still a virgin and felt himself grin at the thought. Only virgins and old librarians walked around with their noses in the air and their mouths all pursed up as if they were tasting something sour.

Michelle, draped in her raincoat, hurried out back in search of Gator. The rain fell in sheets. The wind slapped her coat against her legs and spit mud onto her stockings as she picked her way cautiously across the backyard, trying not to slip in the wet grass. She found Gator sprawled beneath the back of the house. For a moment, all she could do was stare. His slicker had worked its way up around his waist, exposing his jean-clad body from the hips down. And how about those hips, she thought, her gaze fastened to the taut muscles. Her gaze lingered just a moment before moving downward to his lean thighs and calves. And then all at once, those hips started moving, sliding from side to side like a rattlesnake in reverse. There was a loud grunt, and the rest of his body emerged, his big fists gripping several sheets of plywood.

"Well don't just stand there like a bump on a log," Gator said, once he'd spied her. "Help me get this plywood out."

The man had the manners of a goat, Michelle thought. "Just a minute," she said, setting the hammer and box of nails under the house so they wouldn't get wet. She stooped beside him and pulled the plywood out. It was going to be a long day, she thought.

An hour later, Michelle and Gator had managed to board up the two largest windows on the back of the house, although it was next to impossible to work against the fierce wind, despite the protection offered by the screened porch. Several times Michelle found herself flattened against the house, unable to move from the wind's force, while the screens billowed and strained with each gust. One tore loose and spit rain into her face, almost blinding her. Finally, Gator gripped her around the waist with both arms and literally shoved her toward the back door.

"Go inside," he yelled. "I'm going to try and secure my boat."

Michelle didn't argue. She knew she'd only hinder him further because of her inability to fight the wind. She managed to get the back door open, but another wind gust sent water spraying onto the wood floor and onto Reba, who helped close the door behind Michelle.

"Where'd Gator run off to?" she asked, wringing her frail hands.

"He's checking his boat," Michelle said, gasping for breath. "It's bad out there, Grand. Real bad." Michelle noticed for the first time that Reba's hound was standing beside her. "What is Mae West doing out of bed? Shouldn't she be with her puppies?"

"The wind scared her," Reba said. "She can't sit still. And Mister Ed is going bananas." She motioned toward the parrot, whose claws gripped the side of his cage.

The lights flickered and both women looked up with a start. "I need all the tape you can get your hands on," Michelle told her grandmother. "While I tape the windows I want you to look for candles."

Michelle shrugged out of her raincoat but didn't bother to get out of her wet uniform. She went right to work, taping windows as fast as she could. Gator came in a few minutes later, dropped his slicker onto the floor, and assisted. By the time they ran out of tape they'd managed to secure most of the windows on the first floor, as well as the larger ones on the second.

Gator backed away from one of the large plate-glass windows in an upper-story bedroom and surveyed the big X they'd made on the glass with masking tape. "Well, I reckon that's the best we can do."

Michelle saw that he was literally soaked to the skin. His jeans were muddy and plastered against his thighs and calves in a way that made her mouth go dry. His shirt was drenched as well and hung open to his waist, exposing his wide chest, where black hair glistened wetly. His thick hair was slicked to his scalp, giving him a rakish appearance. Michelle realized that she didn't look much better. Her cotton uniform was saturated, and it molded to her body like a second skin. Her nipples, erect from the cold rain and chafing cotton material of her uniform, were clearly visible as they strained against the wet fabric. She blushed profusely when she caught Gator staring. But if she was uncomfortable before, it was nothing compared to the unease she felt when those hooded black eyes locked with her own.

"We need to get out of these wet things," she said, crossing her arms in front of her in an attempt to hide herself. She shivered as Gator continued to stare. He still had the power to make her body go berserk when he looked at her that way, she thought. Those glittering black eyes didn't miss a thing. It was as though he were capable of seeing past flesh and bone to her inner workings, all of which shook at the moment as violently as the tree limbs outside the window. She was certain he knew what that look did to her—what it did to every female, for that matter. He had it down to an art. And if it had had a powerful effect on her at fifteen, it was doubly so now at thirty.

"That's the best idea I've heard all day," Gator said, shrugging out of his shirt. It was cold and felt like wet seaweed against his skin. He mopped his brow and chest with it and ran it across the back of his neck.

Michelle wondered if he had any idea how sensual that simple act was. He was all rippling muscles and taut flesh. Goose pimples stood out on his shoulders and his nipples puckered from the chill in the room. His arms were lean and as brown as the rest of him. The room seemed to shrink in size. Michelle had seen enough male bodies in her job to know that the one before her was one of the best she'd ever laid eyes on.

Gator would have had to be blind not to notice her perusal. The grin he shot her was brazen. "Like what you see, Mic?"

Michelle's head snapped up with a force that almost sent her reeling. Her face flamed. "I was just . . . just . . ."

"Staring?" He looked faintly amused.

He was laughing at her, she thought angrily. She fought the urge to race out of the room. "Don't flatter yourself," she said tersely.

"I don't have to, pretty lady. You just gave me the biggest compliment I've had in a long time, whether you know it or not."

"You haven't changed at all, Gator Landry. I would have thought by now somebody would've knocked some manners into that thick skull of yours."

"And you haven't changed much yourself," he said. "You've still got the prettiest green eyes I've ever seen. Not to mention the cutest rear end. I'd say you have improved with age." He slung his damp shirt around his neck and stepped closer. "I hear you're a nurse now. I remember the first time you told me you wanted to go into nursing. Do you?"

Michelle fought the urge to back away from him. To do so would have been cowardly, and she would sooner bite off her tongue than show Gator she was afraid of him. "How can I forget," she said. "You suggested we play doctor so I could practice on you."

He chuckled. "But you refused."

"That's because I knew what ailed you and didn't want any part of it."

"I think you did."

"You've always been vile and nasty-minded and hell-bent on getting into every girl's britches."

"How come you didn't return the following summer like you promised?"

"Because I refused to make a career of sitting around and waiting for you to crook your little finger at me, that's why."

"You're still crazy about me, aren't you?"

She almost laughed, because at the moment it was just like old times, with Gator trying his darnedest to get a rise out of her and her tossing his words or innuendos right back in his face. Gator Landry had always been able to make her blush and feel things that other boys couldn't.

"Don't be ridiculous, Gator," she said. "I was only fifteen years old at the time. I'm twice that age now, and I hope I've got twice the sense I had back then when I acted on hormones instead of common sense. Besides, you weren't the first man to kiss me. Nor the last."

He cocked his head to the side, as though pondering the thought. "Maybe not. But I'll bet I'm the one you remembered best."

"You're so smug," she said, wishing he wouldn't stand so close. Every nerve in her body was alive with anticipation, and if that anticipation had been sweet at fifteen, it was even more so now that she fully understood where all those feelings and sensations led. She was sensitized to his every move—the way his chest rose and fell, the way his dark lashes fluttered when he blinked, the way his warm breath felt on her cheek. And she had felt his breath on her cheek often—behind the old Sunday school building, standing in the shadows at the Armory Building where they held Saturday night dances, and swimming beside him in the river.

"You know we could all die out here, Mic," he said, his dark gaze resting on her lips. "In another hour, this storm could blow us clear to kingdom come. What d'you say we give each other a little present?"

Michelle didn't know if he was serious or not, but her mouth flew open in surprise at his blatant request. Gator took this as an invitation, and his own mouth suddenly opened over hers, capturing it in a warm kiss. His big arms snaked around her waist and pulled her close, so close that she could feel the hard muscles of his thighs pressing against hers, the wall of his chest crushing her breasts.

The years had not erased the taste of him from her memory. His tongue coaxed her mouth open wider, making gentle forays between her lips that sent her head spinning. His palms slid down the small of her back, cupped each hip, and pulled her tighter against him, cradling her against the base of his thighs, where his arousal was more than evident. Had another man done the same thing, it would have seemed indecent and out of place, but for a man like Gator, it was as much a part of the kiss as his lips. Gator did nothing halfway. And Michelle could only stand there and hang on for dear life, praying her knees would not buckle beneath her.

When he finally raised his head, he was smiling.

"Nothing has changed between us, Mic," he said, his voice soft with invitation. "After all these years, I still want you. Just as badly as I did when we were fifteen and didn't really know what we were doing. It's better when you're older, you know. But this time I refuse to stop after a few hot kisses."

Michelle realized she was gasping. She stepped away quickly, untangling his arms from her waist. "You're crazy, Gator Landry," she said breathlessly.

This seemed to amuse him. "I thought I was vile and nasty."

"That, too," she said. "But you're crazy as a loon if you think I'd get involved with you."

"Who mentioned anything about getting involved?" he said laughingly. He watched her face flame at the remark. Yes, she still thought she was too damn good for him. Perhaps that's why he'd been attracted to her in the first place, because she was unattainable. He could pick and choose from the local girls, but Michelle Thurston had always made him work for her affections.

"You have an enormous ego problem," she said, shaking her head in disbelief. Oh, what she'd give to slap that smug look off his face. But knowing Gator as she did, she wasn't convinced he wouldn't slap her back. She wondered briefly what she'd seen in him so many years ago. And if she lived to be one hundred, she would never understand why the townspeople had gone and made him sheriff. Lord, the people were either crazy or desperate!

"Somehow, we're going to have to get through this storm together," she finally said. "In the meantime, keep your hands to yourself."

He seemed to ponder it. "Okay," he said, nodding in agreement. "I won't touch you unless you ask me to."

Michelle laughed in spite of her rising anger. "You're unbelievable, you know that?"

"So I've been told. And you would have been able to find out for yourself if you hadn't chickened out on me that night. Do we have a deal? I won't be able to concentrate on protecting you and your grandmother from this storm if you keep throwing yourself at me."

He was laughing at her again, she told herself. Actually, he looked as though he could break out into hearty guffaws at any moment. That was one of the things that had always grated on her nerves most, those secret smiles that hinted that he knew something naughty about her. That, and the way he stood too close when he talked. It always made her feel out of breath, as though she'd just run two miles uphill. His eyes would naturally zoom in on the rise and fall of her chest, which, of course, only made it worse. And the way his gaze roamed over her freely, as if he had every right, told her that whatever he was thinking had to be bad, if not downright raunchy.

"I don't believe we're having this conversation,"

she said, "but you've got yourself a deal. I'll stay as far away from you as I can." As though to prove her point, she turned on her heels and fled. And she wondered then, as she took the stairs two at a time, if those black eyes and his kisses weren't much more dangerous than anything the storm could do to her.

Two

By noon, the fierce wind howled and shrieked like a wild animal, and the house shuddered with each violent gust. Dressed in dry clothes that Reba had pulled from an upstairs closet, Gator dickered with a battery-powered radio that produced a great deal of static. He'd cursed fitfully when he'd remembered he'd left his police radio back at the shelter, but then realized it wouldn't have done much good anyway, since he was so far out in the bayou country. He was going to insist that Reba get a telephone after this thing was over. Her family might not be able to convince her, but he would lay the law down to her once and for all and make her have one installed. At her age, with her car running only half the time, she had to have some way of contacting people. It was too easy to forget about her living out here all alone, and he wouldn't always be around to remind folks.

Michelle, wearing pants that were too big and had to be pinned at the waist, gazed through a partially boarded window where the trees outside shook and swayed, as though some great Pandora's box had been opened and had unleased something awful and evil. Tree limbs and debris were tossed against the house, then sucked in another direction. Her ears popped suddenly, signaling a change in pressure that was as frightening as the wind outside.

Gator stepped closer, still holding the radio at his ear. "Better come away from that window," he said. He'd barely gotten the words out of his mouth before something hit the house with such force, it felt as though it had been lifted momentarily from its foundation. Reba, who'd been rocking in her chair frantically for the past hour, stopped and glanced up as the lights flickered once and went out. They were shrouded in near darkness.

"The water is rising," Gator said, going to the window he'd ordered Michelle away from only seconds before. Reba joined him.

"It looks like the end of the world," she said softly, holding a small calico kitten. She looked from Gator to her granddaughter and back, and she appeared to be on the verge of tears. "You were right. We shouldn't have stayed. If anything happens to the two of you, it'll be all my fault."

"Nothing's going to happen," Gator said, anchoring his hands on her frail shoulders reassuringly.

Michelle would've had to be deaf not to catch the gravity of his voice. Once again, she stepped closer to the window. They were drawn to it like moths to a porch light. She tossed Gator an anxious look over her grandmother's head and found him watching her, a thoughtful expression on his face. What could he be thinking, she wondered. Was he sorry now for staying? She couldn't imagine someone like Gator Landry risking his hide for anyone but himself. She suddenly remembered the kiss they'd shared and glanced away quickly. She returned her gaze to the window, where the bayou, usually without current, was now a pulsing, moving thing with ripples and whitecaps. It sort of reminded her of the way her stomach pitched about each time Gator looked at her with those black eyes.

Gator finally insisted they move to the center of the room, away from the windows. For the next couple of hours they waited and listened as reports filtered in on the radio. They lunched on ham and cheese sandwiches and spice cake and made small talk, listening and waiting. Time crept by slowly. While Reba rocked and sang church hymns under her breath, Gator tried to pull Michelle into conversation.

"Remember the time we got caught in that storm at the swimming hole?" he asked.

Michelle slid her gaze in his direction and felt her face grow warm at the memory. "No."

The smile he gave her told her he knew she was lying. "Think for a minute. It'll come back to you. It started lightning, and we had to leave the water."

How could she forget, she wanted to rail at him. She had ended up in the front seat of his old pickup truck, *alone* with him, wearing only her bathing suit and smelling of cheap suntan lotion. Something in her stomach fluttered as she remembered how he'd looked in his bathing trunks that day.

Gator had matured much faster than the rest of the boys his age, and that day, with his naked chest glistening with oil and his wet trunks clinging to him, Michelle had been convinced of that maturity. That was the day Gator had kissed her for the first time, though heaven knew he'd tried a dozen times before. She couldn't remember exactly how it had begun, but all at once she'd found him close, his mouth touching hers tentatively, as if he were half-afraid she'd scurry away like the squirrels had when the rain had begun. But she hadn't. She had raised her lips to his eagerly. That one kiss awakened everything in her body, those gentle stirrings that he had aroused in her the first time she'd seen him had threatened to ignite into something powerful. She had touched his chest, had drawn tiny playful circles in the light coating of oil that covered him, and had watched in wonder as his nipples hardened and grew erect. She had lain in bed that night for hours, thinking about it, wondering what it would have been like had she not put a halt to the kissing that in just a few minutes had grown hot and frantic. And then she'd buried her head under her pillow and squeezed her eyes tightly closed, believing that no fifteen-year-old girl should ever feel the things Gator had made her feel.

"Yes, I remember," she finally said, meeting the

look in his eyes. She wondered if he knew how powerful that look was. It was almost hypnotic. She felt as though she were being pulled toward him, like a small fish being reeled in on a line. "It seems so long ago," she added, thinking out loud. But the memory was so vivid.

"Sometimes it seems like yesterday," he said.

Something slammed against the side of the house, and Michelle jumped as reality closed in with an urgency that made her tremble. The noise heightened, until the whole area sounded like a war zone. Water lapped onto the back porch and seeped under the back door. They tried in vain to mop it up with towels. Mister Ed squawked and flapped his wings while the hound paced the floor nervously. And then, just when Michelle thought she could take no more, the wind and rain stopped and all she could hear was her own frantic heartbeat. All three hurried over to the window and gazed out at the carnage of small trees and limbs and debris. Everything was dead still. She looked at Gator. "Is it over?"

Gator shook his head. " 'Fraid not, Mic. I think it's just the eye passing over."

She liked the way he said her pet name; it always came out sounding like "Meek." She remembered a magnolia-scented night when he'd whispered her name in her ear, his breath hot against her cheek. She'd sneaked out with him on a dare. She remembered him pulling her down beside him on his mother's old-fashioned quilt, placed on a soft mound of sweet-smelling pine needles, a light summer breeze toying with her hair and fanning her body. His usual playful manner had disappeared that night; the teasing was gone. He'd been a man filled with such a passionate need that it had frightened her. Suddenly, they'd no longer been mere fifteen-year-olds experimenting with touch and feel. The slow burning in Michelle's lower belly had blazed into something wild and reckless, teetering out of control. It had jolted her to the soles of her feet. No boy had ever made her feel those things. She had run from him, leapt from the blanket and torn through the woods as though the devil himself were after her. She had slipped back into her grandparents' house soundlessly, but her heart was beating so loud that she'd been half-afraid the walls would come crashing down around her. It would serve her right, she'd told herself over and over. No decent girl would slip out at midnight to be with the likes of Gator Landry.

That was the last time she'd seen Gator, and she was almost thankful when her parents had come for her the next day. She'd put the summer and her three-month relationship with Gator Landry behind her. She'd never even told him good-bye. But she'd figured it was just as well. Gator probably had hated her for running away from him. Or perhaps he'd had a good laugh over it with his friends. She'd vowed not to humiliate herself further where he was concerned. He could have come after her. Part of her had hoped he would.

Michelle forced her thoughts back to the present. Another few minutes passed in absolute silence before Gator decided to venture outside and have a look around. She followed, wearing rubber knee boots to keep dry. Nothing moved. The air was heavy and oppressive, so thick, Michelle was certain she could chew it. They rounded the house and she gasped, finding a great live oak completely unearthed, lying across the back of her new Ford. Her heart sank.

"Well, there goes all hopes of getting out of here," she said, feeling the sting of tears at her eyes. She and Gator stepped closer to survey the damage.

He shook his head but tried to sound optimistic. "Good thing it didn't fall on the front of your car, or it would have crushed your engine."

Michelle laughed hollowly. "What does that matter? It's still a wreck. And I just bought the damn thing." She was crying now, but she didn't care. "I special-ordered that color and had to wait two months to get it. All those months of doing without, saving every dime I could get my hands on. Giving up my vacation days," she added on a heartfelt sob.

Gator felt his gut wrench at the sight of her tears. He could stand anything but a woman's tears. "Aw, Mic, don't cry," he said, draping one arm over her shoulder. "We're lucky to be alive. I can get somebody out here to pull that tree off your car. You can take it to a body shop, and they'll have it looking brand new again. Just be thankful it was your car and not one of us."

Michelle couldn't stop crying no matter how hard she tried. "We could still die," she said, swiping at the tears miserably. "The back side of the storm is supposed to be as bad as the front, if not worse. If something happens to Grand, I'll never forgive myself for not putting my foot down and forcing her to leave."

"I think she had her mind made up, Mic," he said softly. "It won't be anybody's fault."

Michelle hiccuped. "Oh, Gator, I'm so scared. I've never been this scared in my life. And I'm used to seeing unpleasant things. I see them every day as part of my job. I thought I had a grip on it." Tears streamed down her cheeks, fear and exhaustion warring inside her. She closed her eyes, trying to block out the images around her.

Gator hugged her close, feeling his heart swell with concern. He kissed her forehead, her closed eyelids, whispering words of reassurance to her. "You're one of the bravest women I know, Mic," he said at last. "And I'm not going to let this thing hurt you or your grandmother. I'll do anything to keep you safe. Do you understand?"

Michelle opened her eyes. For once there was no sign of laughter or amusement on his face. His look was both tender and sincere. It felt wonderful in his arms, she decided. Secure. She felt safe for the first time in hours. As crazy as it sounded, she *did* trust him, and she knew he would do anything to prevent them from getting hurt.

"Sometimes, I get tired of being brave all the time," she confessed. "People come into the emergency room looking so bad, it's all I can do not to turn and run in the other direction." She swallowed a lump at the back of her throat. "They look at us as if we've got the power to make them live and—" She stopped. "We don't always. They beg us not to let them die, their families beg us to keep them alive, but sometimes we just can't."

"You can only do so much," he said, smoothing her hair back from her face with a big hand. Gator couldn't believe the feeling of tenderness that had welled up in him over her confession. She had always seemed so self-assured, so in control of her feelings. That was one of the reasons why he enjoyed teasing her. He wanted to see if he could crack that cool exterior, make that wall of reserve come tumbling down around her. He had teased and tormented and tried his damnedest to seduce her, but he'd never stood by and watched her heart break into a million pieces. It suddenly became of the utmost importance to protect her and those she loved, and it had nothing to do with duty or what was expected of him. He wanted to keep her safe for himself, in case there was anything left of the relationship they'd begun so long ago. He was still a selfish bastard, he supposed.

Michelle squirmed deeper into his embrace and closed her eyes again, unaware of the effect she was having on him. It had been so long since she'd been held by a man. Everybody needed to be hugged, or simply touched, by another human being from time to time, she told herself. She gave so much of herself to her patients; was it wrong to ask for something in return? She slipped her arms around Gator's waist, and pressed herself against his solid body, wishing to draw upon his strength. She had spent so many years offering strength and nurturing others that it felt wonderful receiving the same for herself.

The storm would return with all its fury before long, and they could very well die, but for now she wanted to bask in the warmth of Gator's embrace. Nothing else mattered at the moment. She was obviously in shock, she told herself. People did strange things when faced with their own mortality. But she forced the thought away, focusing instead on his scent and the way his lips felt in her hair, against her forehead, as he tried to offer comfort.

"Kiss me, Gator," she said, her voice a mere whisper.

He needed no further prompting. Gator lowered his head and captured her lips. Michelle remained as still as the grass and trees surrounding them as his warm mouth opened over hers. His tongue was hot as it forged past her lips and explored her mouth with a thoroughness that left her tingling inside and out. His hands moved to the small of her back, caressing and kneading the tense muscles there while the muscles low in her belly coiled tightly. Although the kiss was as sensual as they come, Michelle sensed something more, an odd, giving sort of thing, almost nurturing, as though Gator were trying to impart a bit of himself as well. She opened her eyes slowly when he raised his head.

"We'd better go back in now," he said at last, though his blood was roaring in his ears. He wanted her more than he'd ever wanted her in his life, and in another five seconds he'd forget where they were and the dangers awaiting them. But he'd promised to protect her, and he had every intention of doing just that. "Reba will be worried."

Michelle nodded dumbly, and with his arms circling her waist protectively, she walked beside him to the house. It was time to wait for the backlash.

The second half of the storm shattered windows, snapped trees in half, and spilled water onto the first floor of the house. Gator, having foreseen the event, had ordered both women upstairs into a short hall where there were no windows. Reba had insisted on bringing the animals up as well, so they huddled together in silence while Mister Ed squawked from his cage, the cats slinked from room to room, and Mae West growled menacingly from her box filled with puppies. Their only light was provided by an old kerosene lamp. Sometime later they dined on cold pork and beans and bread. From time to time, Gator shined his flashlight down the stairwell.

Michelle had avoided talking to him as much as possible once her fear had abated and common sense had returned, along with the jolting realization that she had asked Gator to kiss her. Good grief, she still couldn't believe it! This was a man who no doubt spent his Saturday nights staring into a beer bottle and playing musical beds with any woman who was willing, she reminded herself, and she had played right into his arms. But surely he realized she had been near hysteria at the time.

"What are you looking for?" Michelle finally

asked when Gator checked the stairs again with his flashlight. "Is the water getting higher?" It had already crept to the second stair.

"Rising water isn't the only thing we have to worry about," he said dully, snapping off the light.

"Then what?"

"He's looking for snakes," Reba said matter-of-factly. "Where there's water, there's snakes."

Michelle swallowed. "Snakes?"

Gator nodded. "Cottonmouths."

Michelle could almost taste the fear in her own mouth. She shuddered, then scooted closer to her grandmother, trying to shut out the images around her. Somehow she would get through all this, she promised herself, and tomorrow she'd have someone pull that tree off her car so she could return home. If only the wind and rain would stop. If only the water would go down and take the snakes with it. If only Gator hadn't kissed her and brought back all those disturbing feelings.

When the wind finally died down to a steady whine, Gator insisted they try to rest, since none of them would be going anywhere until morning. After closing the bedroom door and stuffing clothes beneath it to prevent snakes from entering, Gator positioned himself in an old over-stuffed chair while Reba and Michelle shared the antique iron bed and its feather mattress. Michelle was certain she'd never fall asleep, but somehow exhaustion forced her eyes closed. She opened them briefly when she heard Gator scuttling about the room with his flashlight, shining it on the floor and under the bed. But she was too tired to question him. Of course, had she known he was still looking for snakes . . .

Morning came, and with it a beautiful blue sky. Michelle felt her heart soar at the sight of it, and she threw her arms around her grandmother, who gazed out the window beside her, looking very forlorn at the devastation around them.

"We're alive, Grand," she whispered to the distraught woman. "Right now that's all that matters." Gator, wearing a night's growth of beard, offered her a slight smile, and she thought he had never looked sexier. Not that it mattered, she reminded herself. The sooner she got away from Gator and the bayou, the better off she'd be.

They crept down the stairs cautiously, Gator shining the flashlight in front of him. Although the water had gone down a bit, the first floor was soggy. Gator turned to Reba.

"You can't stay here now. You know that, don't you?" The old woman refused to meet his gaze. "There's no electricity, and this place is probably crawling with snakes. I'll try to find my boat, and if it's still in one piece, we'll use it to get out." When she didn't respond he went on. "We can take the hound and her puppies . . . but the cats will have to stay. You can put food and water out, and they'll be fine for a couple of days."

"I can't leave Mister Ed," Reba said. "If there are snakes . . . well, they'd go right for him, you know."

At the sound of his name, Mister Ed squawked

loudly. Gator sighed and shook his head. "Just let me see if I can find the boat first. We'll tackle the other problems when we get to them."

"Where will we go?" Michelle asked.

"There are several shelters in town, but I'm certain they won't allow pets." He paused. "You're welcome to stay at my place—if it's still standing," he said. Then, at the dark look she shot him, he added, "At least until other arrangements can be made." He made his way to the back door, wrenched it open, and glanced out. All at once he laughed.

"What is it?" Michelle hurried over and peered out the door. Gator's boat had somehow come through a screen, and part of it rested on the back porch, which was ankle-deep in water. The propeller had been torn off the motor and was nowhere in sight. One oar floated nearby and Gator grabbed it, knowing it was their only link to civilization.

"Wonder how long it's going to take me to paddle the three of us ten miles up the bayou," he said, his look amused, despite the awful task that lay ahead.

Before Michelle knew what was happening, they were both laughing, great hearty chuckles that brought tears to their eyes. Reba joined them, laughing so hard she got a stitch in her side. The land around them lay in waste, but for the moment they couldn't get past the joy of being alive and unharmed.

By the time Gator and Michelle managed to get the boat off the back porch, Reba had seen to the care of her cats and had boxed what supplies they might need for the trip. They located the other oar floating in the backyard near a shed. The hound and her puppies were loaded into the center of the boat where Reba was to sit, while Michelle sat in the front holding Mister Ed and his cage and feeling ridiculous. Gator shoved off from the back porch and began rowing.

The bayou had changed considerably with the deluge of water, but it presented no problem for Gator, who knew the area like his own bedroom. They rowed while the first reports came in on the radio. New Orleans, it seemed, had received the brunt of the storm; almost a hundred thousand people were without power and thousands were homeless.

At first Michelle was too engrossed in the sights around them to do anything more than stare. Here and there a warbler cried out, the first signs of life stirring after the storm. A bullfrog croaked from somewhere in the distance, and they caught sight of a white-tailed deer standing in the brush looking at them in a dazed fashion. Still holding the birdcage in her arms, Michelle dozed. She awoke to the sound of a steady hum and glanced up as a small helicopter flew overhead. All three waved as the chopper dipped and circled over them, then headed in another direction.

"They'll send somebody after us," Gator said, giving Reba a reassuring smile.

He proved right. Within the hour a large boat rounded a bend of cypress trees. It was a welcome sight to the weary group.

Three

Once they'd been towed to the main pier, where Gator's newer-model pickup truck was parked, Michelle climbed into the back with the birdcage and dogs, feeling very much as if they were Louisiana's version of the Beverly Hillbillies. Gator immediately drove to the nearest shelter, which had been set up in City Hall. He parked his truck under a live oak so the animals would stay cool while they went inside. The mayor looked relieved to see Gator.

"We've been searching high and low for you, boy," he said, his cigar sending out puffy smoke rings over his head, as he completely ignored the NO SMOKING signs along the walls. "I was beginning to think something had happened to you."

Gator briefly explained the situation, but was more concerned about how the small town had fared during the storm. While he and the mayor held a short meeting, Reba and Michelle grabbed a cup of coffee. Sleeping bags littered the floor, several of them holding sleeping babies. Here and there groups of children played with toys while their parents stood nearby. Some were distraught over the situation, others confused.

When Gator returned, looking tired and concerned, Michelle handed him her cup of coffee and he gladly accepted it. "One of our volunteer firemen has offered to drive you and the animals out to my place," he said. "He checked earlier and found it still standing. You're welcome to stay there, but I don't have time to take you myself right now." He glanced around. "As you can see, this place is a bit crowded, as I imagine the other shelters are. The motel down the street is full as well."

Michelle pondered the thought. The last place in the world she wanted to stay was with Gator Landry, but she didn't want to argue the point at the moment with so many other problems to attend to. Besides, they had to do something with Reba's pets.

"Where's the nearest hospital?" she asked. As long as she was there she might as well make herself useful.

"Thirty miles from here. But we have a clinic in town."

"Can you drive me there? They may need an extra pair of hands."

"Yeah, sure."

"I'll ride out to your place then and see to my animals," Reba said. "But if it's okay with you, I'd just as soon come back here. Several of the couples need baby-sitters so they can drive out and check the damage to their homes."

Gator nodded, already moving to the back of the building, with another man in tow. The women followed. Reba's pets were quickly transferred to another vehicle. Michelle hugged her grandmother, then climbed into Gator's truck.

The town had been hit hard, Michelle noted on the drive to the clinic. Power lines were down everywhere. Trees had been toppled, rooftops sheered from houses, metal signs bent or completely torn away. They passed a car that had been turned upside down, its wheels pointing to the sun, looking like a dead insect. The water had not yet receded, but it hadn't stopped the workers, who wore knee-high rubber boots to get around.

"When do you think the telephone lines will be restored?" Michelle asked Gator as he turned onto the main road.

"Hard to tell. We have an emergency line open so the families here can touch base with their relatives. Is there someone you need to call?" He glanced at her. Of course there was, he told himself. Any woman with her looks would have a man waiting somewhere. "A boyfriend, perhaps?" he asked, knowing he wasn't being very subtle in his attempt to find out about her personal life.

Michelle met his questioning gaze. The man certainly had gall, she thought, prying into her personal life as though he had every right. She shrugged and turned away. Let him wonder. Heaven knew she'd spent a lot of time wondering about him in her lifetime. "Perhaps," she said.

Gator tightened his grip on the steering wheel, waiting for her to expound on her answer. When she didn't, he glanced in her direction once more. "Is that a yes or a no?" he finally asked.

Michelle, caught up in the sights around her, shot him a blank look. "What did you say?"

Gator sighed. "I'm just trying to find out if you have a boyfriend, okay?"

"Why?"

"Just curious, that's all."

"I've had my share of boyfriends, yes," she said, wondering if he had picked up on the fact that she was speaking in the past tense. "What do you think I've been doing these fifteen years, sitting in some convent waiting for you to call? You never did call me, you know. Nor did you bother to write." There, she'd finally said it. But she was about fifteen years too late, she reminded herself.

He looked surprised. "You never gave me your address or telephone number."

"You could have gotten it easily enough from Reba."

Gator didn't answer right away. "I really didn't think you wanted me to contact you, Mic. After . . . that night. You took off like a bat out of hell."

"I was scared."

"Of me?"

"Things got out of hand. If I had stayed, we probably would have . . . well, you know."

"Would that have been so bad?"

She swung her head around so that she was looking at him once again. "We were only fifteen years old, for Pete's sake. Of course it would have been bad." She sighed. "I shouldn't have sneaked out with you that night. I was just asking for trouble."

"Why did you?"

"Because I'd never really done anything that daring before. And it had sounded so romantic when you suggested it, sort of like something out of *Romeo and Juliet.* I suppose I was naive. I'm not so naive anymore."

Gator felt silly now for questioning her. He'd been crazy to think she would still be even remotely interested in him. Of course there would have been other men in her life, and maybe there was somebody special now. He knew she wasn't married because Reba complained about it whenever he inquired about her, bemoaning the fact she would never have great-grandchildren. But kissing Michelle had brought back all those sweet memories of how she'd tasted and felt in his arms so long ago. He could only imagine what it would be like to make love to her. It was a bit late to think about those things now, he told himself. "I'll arrange for you to call your boyfriend this afternoon, Mic," he said softly, his voice resigned.

"I can't call him," she said matter-of-factly as Gator pulled into the parking lot of a large clinic. "His wife might object." She wasn't sure what had made her say it, other than the trace of bitterness left inside her over the breakup that had taken place almost six months earlier. She wasn't proud of her rancor; she had always been the type to forgive easily. She'd learned in the emergency room that stressed-out doctors and patients in pain often said things they didn't mean. But this was personal.

Gator didn't respond right away. He parked his truck and turned off the engine. For a moment, he merely gazed at her, studying her profile. She was still about as pretty as they come, he decided. Her skin was flawless except for her nose, which was peppered with light freckles. She met his gaze. Her green eyes were cautious. "I'm sorry, Mic," he said at last.

Michelle arched her brows in surprise. "Sorry?" It wasn't exactly the response she'd expected.

He nodded. "I'm sorry you're involved in something like that."

"I'm not involved anymore," she told him. "I broke it off when he married." She paused. "The woman meant nothing to him. She was a one-night stand who got pregnant and refused to have an abortion. So he . . . Jeffrey . . . did the honorable thing and married her. We're still friends, of course, since we have to work together. I guess I just feel sorry for myself now and then." She stiffened when she caught him smiling. "What's so funny?"

"I just thought it odd that you don't kiss like a woman who's pining away over another man." Gator knew he wasn't being very sensitive, but he couldn't help himself. He didn't want to hear about the man in her life. Maybe he had double standards; Lord knew he'd had his share of women these fifteen years.

Michelle felt the color drain from her face. He was, of course, talking about the kiss they'd shared during the eye of the storm. How like Gator to bring it up now, throw it in her face when she'd just confessed something very personal to him. "That didn't mean anything. I was afraid of dying. I was looking for anything to take my mind off the danger we were in."

Gator's jaw hardened perceptibly. The thought that she might have simply used him because the man she truly cared for was taken, irked him more than he wanted to admit. "Who are you trying to convince, Mic? Me or yourself?"

She wrenched the door open. He was laughing at her again, damn him! He'd shared her most terrifying moment with her, had kissed and held her as she'd struggled with her own fear of a world gone mad around her, and now he was mocking her, holding her up for ridicule. Anger surged through her. "Listen to me, you nasty-minded Cajun," she said through gritted teeth. "I'd sooner drown myself in the bayou than get mixed up with the likes of you."

Gator winced at her words, but he was clearly amused. He had obviously pushed her too far with his comments, but it was encouraging to know he could still rattle her. "Jeeze, Mic, where'd you learn to talk like that?" He didn't wait for her to answer. "And you were such a sweet, shy thing when we met. Now you're stuck on a married man and using foul language. Before I know it you'll be scribbling four-letter words on the bathroom walls."

Michelle climbed out of the truck and slammed the door. "I'm not fifteen years old anymore," she said through the open window. "I've seen the real world. I've worked with victims of drug overdoses, suicides, gang wars. I've seen women beaten beyond recognition and—" She paused and shook her head as though to clear her mind. Why was she telling him all this? "You're the last person in the world to judge me, Gator Landry, when you're out carousing and womanizing. You're unfit to call yourself sheriff of this town. Not only that—"

"There's no need to go on," he said, his eyes bright with humor. "I think you've established your feelings toward me." He started his engine. "But right now I have to get back to my duties. I may be a lousy sheriff, but I'm all these people have at the moment." He put the truck into gear and drove away, leaving Michelle standing in the parking lot feeling foolish. She'd always said and done foolish things when Gator was around. She would have thought she'd have grown out of it by now.

The staff at the clinic seemed relieved to have her there. One of the nurses found her a clean change of clothes, handed her a bucket of water, and showed her where she could wash up. The clinic, just like City Hall, had a backup generator, which meant there were lights. The storm had taught her a new appreciation for the simple luxuries, she thought as she emerged from the washroom fifteen minutes later feeling refreshed, her long hair combed and tied back at her neck.

Thankfully, there had been no deaths, although some of the people from the mobile-home park had been injured severely enough to be sent on to the hospital. An elderly man was brought in that afternoon with head injuries and a fractured leg. He'd been trapped under a collapsed building all night, and his condition was critical. While the doctor and his nurse stabilized him, Michelle assisted by applying a temporary leg splint. Once his vital signs improved, he was put into an ambulance and driven to the hospital. The staff spent the remainder of the day treating minor injuries, fractures, and strained backs.

When Gator arrived back at the clinic at the end of the day, he found Michelle in the lounge eating a hot dog, drinking coffee, and looking as tired as he felt. A couple of the restaurant owners in town had donated food that would have gone bad with no refrigeration. She offered him one of the hot dogs, and he accepted it, suddenly realizing he hadn't eaten all day. It had been one of the most grueling days of his life, searching through rubble for bodies. He'd found none, for which he was grateful. He'd deputized the fire department and placed the men in town to prevent looting.

"Do you need to hang around here?" Gator asked. "You look as though you could use a rest."

She nodded. "I am tired. The reception room has been packed all day, but I think everything is under control now."

"Why don't we drop by City Hall, pick up Reba, and go to my place," he suggested. "I think we deserve a break after what we've been through."

"That would be nice." She wadded up her hot dog wrapper and tossed it in a nearby trash can. She still didn't relish the thought of staying at Gator's, especially after their argument earlier, but at the moment she didn't seem to have much choice. "Just let me clear it with the others," she said, hurrying out of the room.

Ten minutes later they were on their way to City Hall. Neither of them spoke, and Michelle wondered if Gator felt as uncomfortable as she did. She decided she had better clear the air if she was going to be spending the night at his place.

"Look, I'm sorry about what I said earlier," she sputtered without preamble. She saw Gator's look of surprise and went on. "I don't know why I got so bent out of shape. Stress, I guess. This whole thing has turned me upside down."

Gator shrugged. "I reckon I had it coming. Sometimes I don't know when to stop pushing. But everybody is feeling kind of jittery right now."

"I'd like the two of us to be friends, " she said, "since it looks as though we're going to be spending the next couple of days together." She glanced away. "There's no reason to harbor bad feelings over something that happened fifteen years ago."

Gator knew that she was right, that they should put their differences aside. And he *had* been holding a grudge all these years, he realized. When she'd run away from him that night, he'd thought the worst, that maybe he had disgusted her. Or that his lack of experience had made him appear awkward or clumsy in her eyes. She was a big-city girl, straight out of Baton Rouge, where, he'd been certain, the guys his age were more sophisticated and knew how to make women feel good. He was a yokel, a hillbilly, who knew very little about French kissing or foreplay.

When Michelle had pushed him away and run,

he figured he was sorely lacking in the romance department.

He couldn't believe she didn't even say good-bye, and he couldn't bring himself to ask Reba for her address. What would a good-looking city girl want with the likes of him? he'd wondered. She'd probably laughed at him. Besides, he was only fifteen years old, with high school in front of him. What could he have offered her?

Gator forced his thoughts back to the present. Michelle was looking at him, waiting for an answer. She wanted to be friends. How could a man be friends with the girl he'd first loved? he wondered. Well, he would try anything once. "Sure, I'll be your friend," he said, breaking for a stop sign. "Why not?" It was crazy to expect more from a woman who was carrying a torch for another man.

Michelle smiled. "Good, let's shake on it." She offered her hand.

Taking her hand in his was his first mistake, Gator realized the minute his fist closed over hers. He almost jumped, and felt as if two raw wires had just made contact. The effect was immediate, sending powerful currents up his arms, and he was certain the hair along his forearm was standing on end. He released her, but he could still feel the small imprint of her hand in his palm. He gripped the steering wheel tightly and drove on, but he could not take his mind off how it had felt to hold that dainty hand, or how that hand would feel on his body in a loving caress. It was clear to him he could not touch her without wanting her.

Michelle would have had to be blind not to notice the change in Gator. She, too, was shaken. How could an innocent handshake have such a powerful effect on her? she wondered. This had nothing to do with mere friendship, she decided. His hand closing over hers had conveyed much more. She could imagine those leather-roughened hands on her skin. Those hands could yield strength and power or stroke a woman with a touch as light as dandelion fluff. The knowledge only heightened her awareness of him, and she wondered if there was a woman alive who was not susceptible to the very maleness of him.

Michelle returned to the shelter with Gator. But before they picked up Reba, she helped administer to several people with minor injuries.

It was late when Gator drove Michelle and Reba to his place, which turned out to be a blue, forty-foot-long houseboat located in a cove on Hell Hole Bayou. Surprisingly enough, it had sustained very little damage from the storm, except for a shattered window and some water leakage. His power was out, but that was the norm.

Using his flashlight to guide them, Gator helped Reba and Michelle out of the truck and led them onto the deck of the houseboat. He stopped at the door long enough to unlock it, then shined the light in so they could pass through first. "Watch your step," he cautioned as they stepped through the doorway. "Just stay where you are till I find my kerosene lamp."

As soon as they had light, Reba checked her

hound and accepted Gator's offer to take the dog out. Mister Ed began to squawk at the sight of them, but was quickly calmed by Reba's voice. She draped a towel over his cage, and he went to sleep.

Michelle found herself standing in a living room of sorts, which was separated from a small kitchen by a counter. The living room furniture consisted of two sofa beds across from which stood a built-in bookcase holding a television and stereo. The bookcase was filled with paperbacks and record albums, but it was too dark to see the titles. She held the lamp up to the entrance of a short hallway and found a small bedroom with an attached bath. Everything was surprisingly neat.

Reba yawned and stretched. "I'm so tired I could drop right here on the floor and it wouldn't matter." Michelle nodded, just as Gator came through the door with the dog.

"I found a couple of flashlights behind the seat in my truck," he said, testing them to make sure they worked. He handed each of them one. "Maybe they'll keep you from bumping into walls. You two can have the bed, and I'll take the couch," Gator said. "But first"—he paused and glanced at Reba, his look amused—"I'd better change the sheets."

Reba merely chuckled, but Michelle rolled her eyes heavenward. "We'd appreciate it very much," she said, sarcasm ringing loud in her voice. Heaven only knew what kind of unnatural acts he'd performed on those sheets.

In the end, Michelle helped him change the sheets, all the while refusing to meet his gaze, which she knew was bright with silent laughter. The man was totally without scruples, she decided. She was thankful it was dark and he couldn't see the bright blush on her cheeks.

"Would you like to wash up?" Gator asked as soon as they'd finished making the bed. "I have several jugs of water in the back of my truck. And I always keep a couple of toothbrushes on hand in case I have company."

"Yes, I'll just bet you do," Michelle replied.

Her words seemed to amuse him even more. "Just let me find you and Reba something to wear, and I'll get the water."

While Reba changed in the bedroom, Michelle poured water into the bathroom sink and bathed her face and the back of her neck, then washed as best she could. Gator passed them a package of toothbrushes through the door, and Michelle took great delight in brushing her teeth for the first time in two days. Maybe she was being too hard on the man, she decided. He was going out of his way to make them comfortable, and it was none of her business what he did with his personal life. He'd worked tirelessly throughout the day to get the town back on its feet, despite the fact that he'd never wanted the job. She had to give him credit for that.

For her, helping others had been a conscious act of meeting her own needs. With her parents so heavily involved in their medical-supply business, which took them all over the country, she'd spent a lot of time with baby-sitters. And without brothers and sisters, there was a certain amount of loneliness involved. She'd admired her parents' business skills, but she'd been more impressed with the doctors and nurses she met through their dealings and the gentle one-on-one relationships that existed between the medical professionals and their patients. Her parents had suggested medical school, which they were certainly able to afford, but she had not been interested in becoming a doctor, who was in her opinion a mere figurehead of the medical profession. It was the nurses who made the difference, she decided. They were the ones who did all the hand-holding, who soothed patients' fears and reassured them in the middle of the night. By becoming a nurse, she had fulfilled both other people's needs and her own.

It was only later that Michelle realized it wasn't enough. Jeff Rigsby was fresh out of medical school, ready to conquer the world. He wasn't hardened like the older doctors—he genuinely cared about his patients. Michelle had caught him crying in the supply room once after losing a young boy they'd worked on for hours, and she had held him for a moment. It had drawn them closer together, so close, in fact, that he often turned to her with his problems. She was only too glad to be there for him. He gave so much of himself that it was only fitting she console him and be his anchor of support when things got tough. And when he'd kissed her one morning after a particularly grueling night in emergency, the bond had grown stronger. This was love, she decided. It didn't matter that there weren't fireworks or bells going off in her head. It was the bonding of two human beings who, each in his or her own way, were trying to make a better world. It did not matter that their lovemaking was not the stuff that made up erotic literature. It was gentle and pleasurable, like a soothing balm to a weary soul. And when he'd confessed his brief fling with the nurse in radiology, she'd forgiven him. Besides, she'd thought she had what mattered most—his trust and deep friendship. Sex was highly overrated in a relationship, she'd decided.

When he'd told her about the baby and his decision to marry the woman, she'd had no choice but to break off their relationship. Still, she'd remained his friend. The pain in his eyes was proof that he'd suffered enough. She'd had to put away the hurt and concentrate on being strong, his "tower of strength," as he often called her. There would be no more intimacy, she told him, because her sense of right and wrong would not allow it. But she would always be there for him to talk to.

In the beginning it had been difficult. She had dreamed of a future with him. They had common interests and goals, and they both wanted children one day. But now another woman would carry those children. It wasn't fair, Michelle told herself when she passed the woman in the nurses' lounge or hallway, watching her waistline thicken with each passing month. She had not realized until then how much she longed for a child, to have the family she'd never had growing up. But it was not to be. Thankfully, the pain had eased over the ensuing months, but not the feeling of rejection and betrayal. She would not make the same mistake again.

When Michelle finally came out of the bathroom, she found Reba already in bed, fast asleep. She changed into the cotton shirt Gator had given her and laughed at the size of it. The hem almost reached her knees, and the sleeves were at least six inches too long. She rolled them up to her elbows. Gator tapped lightly on the bedroom door and she opened it.

"You finished with the toothpaste?" he said.

"Oh, sorry, I'll get it for you." Michelle retrieved it from the bathroom and carried it into the kitchen, where Gator was washing up at the sink. He'd stripped off his shirt and was in the process of soaping his chest, stomach, and underarms. Michelle was riveted to the spot, unable to pry her gaze from him. His jeans rode low on his hips in a way that made her mouth go dry. No matter what she thought of him personally, he was undoubtedly one of the finest-looking men she'd ever laid eyes on. She knew men, Jeff included, who spent hours at the gym but didn't come close to looking so good. She wondered if Gator worked out, but she didn't think so. She could imagine him chopping wood or swimming in the river to stay in shape, but she couldn't envision him lifting weights or running an asphalt track in expensive sweats.

"Would you pass me that towel?" Gator asked, leaning over the sink as he rinsed the soapy foam from his body with a washcloth. It was one of the most sensual acts she'd ever seen.

Michelle reached for the towel on the counter

and handed it to him. He dried himself briskly, then draped the towel around his neck. "Are you hungry?"

Michelle shrugged. It was all she could do to keep her eyes off his chest, the way the blue-black curls glistened in the lamplight, the way his nipples beaded in the cool night air. "A little," she finally said. But mostly she was tense, all wound up, no doubt from all the coffee she'd drank that evening—and from spending so much time with him, she thought.

"All I have is beer and pretzels. You don't impress me as a beer drinker." He'd never been much of a beer drinker himself until he'd worked in the sugar cane fields. It had become a habit to share a cold beer with the rest of the men at the end of a long, hot day. He couldn't drink like most men; it was his metabolism, he supposed. Three beers wouldn't get him drunk but would certainly give him one hell of a headache the following day. The guys at the Night Life Lounge teased him unmercifully about it, and got a kick out of it when, after a couple of brews, he ordered diet soda.

"Right now anything sounds good," Michelle said. She hoped the beer would relax her. Although she was exhausted, she was not ready to climb into bed with her grandmother, whom she knew snored louder than a jumbo jetliner.

Gator reached into the small refrigerator and pulled out two beers. "They're still cool," he said, putting one metal can to his forehead. He popped the metal top on one and handed it to her, then reached inside a cabinet for a bag of pretzels.

Michelle took a seat at the counter and sipped her beer slowly, gazing across at Gator in the dimly lit room. The flame from the lamp painted shadows across his dark face. He leaned on the counter, his elbows propped beneath him, his chin anchored on one fist.

"After watching you tonight, I see why you decided to become a nurse," he said. "You have a calming effect on people." Except on him, he thought. Every nerve in his body came alive when she was near. "I suppose it's a bit dull working in this place after the excitement of working in a big-city hospital."

"Not dull, just different. I'm probably more sympathetic to these people, because they can't help what happened to them. Many of the people I work with at home are responsible in some way for their own injuries or deaths."

"Oh, we have our share of problems here," Gator said. "Domestic violence, drunk drivers, fights."

"Is that why you decided to become sheriff?" She knew it wasn't, but for some reason she wanted to hear it from him.

He straightened and folded his arms over his chest. "I became sheriff because I was elected. I've never had any grand illusions about trying to change the world. I don't really care what goes on around me as long as it doesn't interfere with my life. To someone like you, that probably sounds selfish, but that's the way I am. What you see is what you get."

"Why do you think you were elected in the first place?"

"Because my father was sheriff for so long. Folks just expect me to take over where he left off, I reckon."

"I understand the people thought a great deal of him."

"Yes, and they never fail to remind me how great he was. And now that he's dead it's like he's a national hero or something. You can't compete with somebody like that. But I have more important plans for my life than playing Andy of Mayberry, and the sooner I find somebody to take my place, the better off we'll all be."

She nodded. "Do you plan to live here for a while?" she asked, glancing around.

"Yeah, until I find something else I want to do."

Michelle didn't think it sounded very ambitious, but once again she reminded herself it was none of her business. She stood. "Well, I guess I'd better get some sleep," she said. "Tomorrow is going to be a long day. I don't suppose you have any idea when I can get someone to pull that tree off my car." She hadn't wanted to bother him with it earlier, since he'd been so busy.

Gator regarded her, a half-smile playing on his lips. He wondered if she knew how sexy she looked in his shirt, with her hair hanging loose. "You in a hurry to get back, Mic?" he asked.

"Well I *do* have a job there, you know."

He nodded thoughtfully. "You're sure it doesn't have something to do with your old boyfriend?"

The question surprised her. "Of course not. But that doesn't mean I'm not concerned about him."

Gator rounded the counter, closing the distance between them. He gazed down at her thoughtfully. Without thinking, he reached for a blond curl and rubbed it between his fingers. "He doesn't deserve your concern, Mic. If you and I were sharing the same bed, there wouldn't be another woman carrying my baby." He raised the curl to his mouth and brushed it across his full bottom lip. "I like to keep my sleeping arrangements simple. That way nobody gets shot."

He knew he was totally out of line for saying such a thing, but jealousy was eating at his gut and he couldn't help it. He had no claim on her, but the mere thought of her loving another man made him crazy. He had thought of her over the years, but the pictures he'd conjured in his mind—her leaning over a sick patient or lunching with the other nurses in the hospital cafeteria— had never included another man. It wasn't what he truly believed, he realized now. He'd simply been fooling himself.

Michelle didn't know what to say at first. His words had caught her off guard. She could only gaze at his eyes, which looked like glittering onyx in the dim light. Her heart was pounding so loud, she was afraid he heard it. She pulled her hair from his grasp. "Are you trying to tell me you're a one-woman man, Gator?" she asked once her senses had returned. She didn't give him a chance to respond. "Because if you are, let me assure you I don't believe it. You with that . . . that hickey on your neck."

He grinned. "It's not a hickey, Mic."

"Yeah, right." Her voice was edged with sarcasm.

This time he chuckled softly. "It's a bee sting,

darlin'. I had an allergic reaction. But don't get me wrong: I'm not opposed to having a woman give me a love bite. I just prefer they do it where it doesn't show. No sense advertising what I do in bed. Know what I mean?"

She didn't know whether to believe him or not. "Why didn't you say something this morning? You let me believe the worst."

"I did it because I love to see you get riled. Just like I let you believe I'd had some woman tangled up in my sheets last night and had to pull them off the bed before you caught something. I didn't want to ruin your bad impression of me by letting you think I was only trying to be a good host. You see, my mama taught me a long time ago that I should have clean sheets and towels when company came. As well as a new toothbrush. But it was more fun watching your imagination run away with you."

"You did it because you enjoy laughing at me."

His look sobered. "I'd never laugh at you, Mic."

Michelle swallowed. She wondered if she would ever be able to hold a conversation with him without her emotions running the full gamut. One minute he was teasing her, the next he was charming her socks off, and at a moment's notice he would turn thoughtful and sincere. The man was full of contradictions. She couldn't keep up with him. Perhaps that's how he operated—he confused the woman, then made his move. She pitied the poor woman who got involved with him. A relationship with Gator would be stormy and unbalanced, filled with peaks and valleys, never smooth-running.

"I have to go to bed now," she said, feeling the need to put some distance between them. She felt vulnerable with him, and it made her uncomfortable. Although he held up his end of the conversation as well as the next person, she was constantly aware that just below that thin line of conventionality, there was a very potent man who exuded raw masculinity and knew precisely what buttons to push when dealing with a female. She missed the easygoing, uncomplicated relationship she'd had with Jeff.

"G'night, Mic," he said softly.

Michelle turned for the bedroom, but she could feel his gaze on her. She didn't feel safe until she was inside the room with the door closed behind her. But sleep was a long time coming. Every time she closed her eyes, she saw Gator's face. Gator Landry was dangerous, she told herself. He had promised to protect her from the storm, but who was going to protect her from him and these feelings she had every time he was near?

Four

The Red Cross arrived two days later with tents and donated items, most of which were used for those families who'd lived in the mobile-home park that had been virtually destroyed. Water and ice and various other food supplies began coming in on trucks, so that people's immediate needs were met. Gator and the town's other officials had combed the area, sifting through debris, while Michelle had divided her time between the clinic and shelters. Gator had also checked on Reba's cats, putting out bags of food and fresh water and performing what he called the "god-awful task" of changing their kitty litter. Although the water had gone down somewhat, he cautioned Reba about returning too soon.

When Michelle was finally able to get through to the hospital, she found her co-workers frantic but more than understanding that she could not return right away, especially when her car was still buried under a tree. The hospital was under-staffed since they'd sent medical personnel to New Orleans, and when Michelle spoke with Jeff, she learned he'd been pulling double shifts right along with everyone else. He sounded exhausted and a bit irritated that she hadn't called sooner.

"We've tried to find out about you several times, Michelle," he said. "All they told us was there had been no casualties. But nobody knew if you were injured, and you didn't tell any of us your grand-mother's name."

"I'm sorry, Jeff," she said, feeling guilty for making everyone worry so. Heaven knew, Jeff had enough to deal with at the moment, what with a new wife who was pregnant. "You have to wait your turn to use the phone's here, because we only have a couple of lines open. And in the begin-ning I was more concerned with taking care of the emergencies." She paused. "You sound dead on your feet."

"I am. I've been sleeping at the hospital every night, and you know what that's like. But it beats the heck out of going home. It's not working out, Michelle. I made a mistake. I don't know how long I can take it."

She was genuinely sorry for him. The man had tried to do the honorable thing by marrying the woman, and she knew he was paying emotionally. "Just hang in there, Jeff," she said. "I'll be home in a couple of days and we'll talk."

"What kind of life is this, Michelle?" he said, sounding on the verge of tears. "All I do is work. My patients don't appreciate me—they want more. They're takers, Michelle. And then I have to go home to a wife who despises me and is sick all the time. There's no payoff, no joy in my existence. I can't take much more."

Michelle was growing irritated with his whining. "Don't talk like that, Jeff," she said firmly, wondering when he'd first started acting like a cry baby. He was a grown man—a doctor, for heaven's sake! Perhaps his work in emergency was taking its toll. "You're stronger than you think. This has been a bad time for you, but you'll get through it." She glanced over her shoulder to where a group of people had congregated at the door, each of them anxious to use the telephone. "Look, Jeff, I have to get off. People are waiting to use the phone."

"When are you coming home?"

"As soon as I can. I promise. Good-bye, Jeff." She hung up the telephone, shaking her head, wondering if life would ever return to normal.

"Everything okay?" Gator asked, noting the worried expression on her face.

Michelle didn't speak until she was out of hearing distance from the others. "I need to go home, Gator," she said as soon as he'd joined her.

"Let the guy work out his own problems, Mic."

"I don't expect you to understand."

"I understand a man has to take responsibility for his own actions. Stand on his own two feet. You're not his mother."

She didn't appreciate him sticking his nose in her business. "I happen to be his friend. What would you do, Gator, turn your back on him?"

"His problem has nothing to do with you. It's between him and his wife."

Her anger flared. "You have no right to pry into my personal life, and you certainly have no right to pass judgment on a man like Jeff. What do you know about honor and obligation? You can't wait to dump your own responsibilities into somebody else's lap and go on with your life. Jeff didn't have that choice."

"I told you before, everybody has choices. I think he made his."

Michelle had never known Gator to be cruel, not even at his angriest. What did he hope to prove? She had come to terms with her relationship a long time ago; in fact, there were times she wondered what she had even seen in Jeff. But Gator had no right to rub her nose in her mistakes, and he certainly had no right to hurt her.

"I'm not going to discuss this with you," she said, holding her hand up to halt the conversation. "But I really need to get back home. If you won't help me find someone to get that tree off my car, I'll do it myself."

Gator realized now that he'd been too rough on her. Once again he'd let his emotions get the best of him. He wanted to apologize for hurting her feelings, kiss away the pain, but it wasn't the place. "The heavy equipment is needed elsewhere at the moment, Mic, you know that. And what are you going to do about your grandmother? Somebody has to help her get her place in order. She's too old to do it alone."

Michelle buried her face in her hands. She was so tired. She was tired of living on stale hot dogs and black coffee. She was tired of wearing the same clothes and of washing her bra and panties in Gator's sink every night. But she knew he spoke the truth: Somebody had to help Reba. With her parents out of the country till the end of the month, she was the only one Reba had to rely on. But that was the story of her life. Her parents had never been around, not for her or anyone else.

Michelle dropped her hands to her side. "Can you take me out to Reba's place tomorrow?" she asked. "I'd like to get started right away."

"Okay, Mic. Lord knows, I wouldn't want you to hang around any longer than necessary." He walked away with a disgusted sigh. Jealousy, he decided, was truly the monster it was reported to be. He hoped for his sake this was his first and last brush with it.

Reba's place was a disaster. Gator and Michelle arrived early the next morning in his boat. Although Reba's house could be reached by car, the distance was much longer that way. Reba had lost two outbuildings, and the screens on her back porch flapped in the breeze like laundry on a clothesline. A number of windows had been shattered, and tree limbs and various other debris littered the yard, giving it an unkempt appearance that was alien to Reba's way of life. Her boat dock and part of the backyard were still covered with water, but for the most part it had subsided.

The inside of the house wasn't much better, and Michelle was thankful that Gator had convinced Reba to stay at his mother's house for a couple of days. Michelle planned to return there as well that evening. Gator's mother had not seemed to mind Reba's pets, and Michelle thought it was high time Reba reacquainted herself with her old friends. The woman had become a recluse since the death of her husband.

"I don't know where to begin," Michelle said, taking in her surroundings. The large braided rug in the living room was soggy, as were the numerous throw rugs scattered across the plank floors. She faced Gator. "You don't need to be here," she said. "I appreciate it, but I know you have more important things to do in town." She didn't know how she would manage without his help, but she felt guilty for taking up so much of his time already.

"Don't worry about it, Mic. I've deputized half the town. They can spare me for a day or two."

"Why are you doing this?" she finally asked. Gator didn't seem the type to go out of his way for another human being unless he was motivated by guilt or obligation. He owed her nothing. Although he'd worked nonstop the past few days since the storm had hit, she knew that he really didn't want to be there, that he was merely biding his time.

Gator shrugged. "It's the least I can do. The people in this town looked after my mother when I moved away. I'd come back to check on her from time to time and find someone had chopped wood or weeded her garden and flower beds for her. I reckon it wouldn't kill me to return the favor." He pressed the toe of his boot against the large rug, and water streamed across the floor. "First thing we need to do is get this rug out of here so the floor can dry."

Michelle sensed he was eager to get started and didn't want to waste time arguing. For the next half hour, they concentrated on getting the rug outside, where they draped it across several old sawhorses to dry. Michelle wasn't sure the rug could be saved, but knowing Reba never threw anything away, she was hesitant to do so herself.

Although it was still early, the day was hot and muggy. Gator, already drenched with perspiration, had shrugged out of his shirt and tied an old blue bandanna around his forehead. A fine sheen of sweat covered his back and shoulders, and tiny sweat beads glistened in his chest hair. That, combined with his unshaven face, convinced Michelle that he'd never looked more rakish or devilishly sexy.

A shave and shower these days would have been sheer luxury, she knew. Although Gator had conveniently disappeared each night during the bath rituals to give Reba and Michelle privacy, there was still something very intimate about sharing the same bar of soap, the same tube of toothpaste, the same sink. Gator often waited until the women were in bed before he began his own ablutions, and Michelle had raptly listened to the sounds he made—the water splashing against the metal sink, Gator humming under his breath as he washed. In her mind she saw him standing naked before the sink, the kerosene lamp painting shadows on his large, hair-roughened body. She wondered how she would ever manage to fall asleep on one of those hard cots in the nurses' lounge again.

Michelle forced her thoughts to the present as she followed Gator inside the house once more. They threw open the windows—those that hadn't been broken during the storm—to aid in drying out the place. Michelle began the enormous task of mopping while Gator measured the windows and cut plastic from a large roll they'd purchased from the hardware store that morning. He had no idea when someone could get out to replace the glass and the plastic covering would at least keep the mosquitoes out. Michelle had only finished mopping half the living room floor when Gator called for her help.

"I need you to hold these plastic sheets in place while I nail them up," he said, rolling the sheets up so they would be easier to handle. He grabbed a hammer and a handful of nails. "Why don't we start upstairs?" Michelle nodded and followed.

Gator had Michelle hold the plastic against the window while he tacked it to the frame securely. Michelle decided it was the most unnerving moment in her life having to stand there, stretched to her full height as she held the plastic in place, while he stood directly behind her and tacked it in. She could feel his breath on the back of her neck, causing the hairs to stand on edge, sending delightful tingles down her back. When his big chest brushed her shoulder blades accidentally, she sucked in her breath and tried to make herself smaller. She suddenly felt vulnerable dressed in shorts that were a tad tight and a cotton blouse that exposed her midriff every time she raised her arms. They'd seemed practical enough when she'd chosen them at the shelter; with clothing so scarce, she'd been lucky to find something close to her size. She decided after a moment that clothing had nothing to do with the way she felt. Gator Landry could make a woman in a nun's habit feel naked.

He smelled of soap and male flesh, and as his powerful arms sent a tack in with one easy blow, the muscles in them flexed. When Gator finally finished nailing the plastic in place, he dropped his arms to his side and backed away from the window. Michelle, who'd been literally holding her breath, exhaled with such force, it almost made her dizzy. She grasped the windowsill for support.

"You okay?" Gator asked, arching one brow quizzically.

"Yeah, fine."

"How come your face is so red, then?"

She fumbled for a reply. "It's the . . . heat."

"I hope you're not pregnant too."

Michelle faced him. "Of course I'm not pregnant. What on earth would make you say such a thing?"

He shrugged. "I just thought it would be kind of funny if Dr. Kildare knocked up his wife and mistress at the same time."

Her cheeks flamed. "I'm not his mistress."

"Call it what you like, Mic, but it all adds up to the same thing."

This time it took every ounce of willpower she had to keep from flying into a rage. "I am *not* sleeping with him," she said. "Not that it's any of your business, but we haven't . . . uh . . ."

"Had sex?"

"Been intimate in months," she managed, feeling more and more flustered with every breath she took. "And I don't have mere sex with any man. If I don't care deeply for someone, I don't sleep with him."

He chuckled. "So that explains the bitchy behavior and those lines on your forehead. You obviously need some good lovin'. And it just so happens I can fit you into my schedule at the moment."

Michelle crossed her arms and regarded him with an air of contempt. "There you go again," she said. "Just when I'm beginning to think your morals have crept a bit higher than a snake's belly, you do your darnedest to prove me wrong."

He looked amused. "Wouldn't want to disappoint you, darlin'."

She smiled sweetly. "You could never do that, Sheriff, because my opinion of you was fairly low to begin with."

Gator stepped closer. "I seem to remember a time when it wasn't so low, Mic. In fact, you were crazy about me that summer."

"I was bored and had nothing better to do."

He smiled, remembering that night so many years ago. "I remember you lying in my arms in the cool, sweet-smelling grass."

"We were on your mother's quilt."

"Beneath a giant live oak."

"It was a magnolia tree."

The smile changed to a grin. "For somebody

who was bored out of her mind, you certainly remember it well."

Michelle blushed. "I have an excellent memory. I never forget a thing."

"Remember what you whispered in my ear that night?"

She glanced away and swallowed. "No."

He tilted his head forward so that she was looking directly into his eyes. "You said I made you feel things you'd never felt before."

"Gator Landry, you're a liar! I never said such a thing."

He nodded slowly. "Oh, yes you did." He crooked a finger beneath her chin and raised her face. "We were both so hot that night, I thought we'd catch fire and burn."

His voice was low but smooth, a liquid purr to her ears that made her mouth go dry and the back of her throat itch. Michelle could only gaze into the onyx eyes that held her so totally captivated. "I keep reminding you that was a long time ago," she finally said. "I don't think I actually realized what I was getting into until you pulled me down on that portable bed of yours. But now I'd just as soon forget it, if you don't mind."

He cocked his head to the side as though pondering her request. "I don't think we can forget it, Mic," he said honestly. How was he supposed to forget the way she'd felt that night when she insisted on cavorting around in those too-short shorts? And where had she found that blouse, for Pete's sake? Every time she took a breath the hem shimmied up her rib cage and he caught sight of peach-colored flesh. He'd almost lost it when he'd spied that kissable navel riding her waistband. He dropped his finger from her chin and rested his hand on her shoulder.

Gator slid his knuckles back and forth across her collarbone reflectively, and the welcoming warmth of his touch seeped through her cotton blouse. "And I don't think we'll ever stop wondering what it would be like between us now, if only we could stop playing games with each other and face our feelings. If we were that volatile at fifteen, what do you think we'd be like now?"

Michelle backed away, wanting to escape the feel of his hand on her. But even as she broke physical contact with him, the impact of his touch lingered. His words had painted a picture in her mind that was much too dangerous to even contemplate. What he was suggesting was crude and indecent, as far as she was concerned. What about love or caring or all the other things that made up a relationship? She almost laughed out loud at the thought. Gator Landry had made it plain from the beginning that he didn't desire a relationship. He was merely looking for a bed partner to entertain him until he could move on. Well, he could look elsewhere, she told herself.

"Are the women in Lizard Thicket getting so scarce that you have to harass every woman who comes into town?" she asked.

"Not at all."

Michelle gritted her teeth at the smug look on his face. The man certainly had a high opinion of himself. "Then why don't you find somebody who's a bit more susceptible to your charms, instead of forcing yourself on someone who isn't?"

He grinned, showing perfect white teeth. "I like you, Mic. You've got style. I like classy women, as long as they don't carry it as far as the bedroom."

Gator turned before she had a chance to respond and reached for another sheet of plastic. He was purposely goading her, he knew, but he couldn't help himself. He enjoyed watching her get so flustered she couldn't think straight. She was fumbling for a comeback even now, and it delighted him that she was having trouble forming a reply. He was aware that his playful banter irritated the dickens out of her, but he couldn't help himself. Part of it, he knew, was to get back at her for wanting to return home so badly. Although she claimed it was her job she was concerned about, he wondered just how much of it actually had to do with the man who'd once been in her life. It irked him that she had fallen for a doctor. But he could see her playing the demure doctor's wife, attending charity functions, raising yellow-haired kids with perfect teeth. He gritted his own teeth at the thought.

Michelle didn't quite know how to respond to his comment, so she said nothing. To respond would merely keep their argument alive, and that, in her opinion, was a waste of time. Let Gator think what he wished of her. She was there for one thing—to see after her grandmother. The sooner she finished, the sooner she'd be on the highway to Baton Rouge.

*   *   *

They worked nonstop the rest of the day, halting only briefly to eat the lunch Reba had prepared that morning.

It was still early when they packed the boat to head home, but Gator wanted to make sure they got in before dark. A man could get lost forever on the bayou at night, he knew.

The house was, for the most part, habitable, although the grounds were still in bad shape, despite all Gator had done. They decided to come back the following day and try to finish up so Reba wouldn't have to worry about it when she returned. While Gator loaded the boat, Michelle put out fresh food and water for the cats and changed the litter boxes. She was on her way out the back door when she spied Gator standing dead still, one arm rigidly extended toward the ground, his pistol aimed at something. She sucked her breath in sharply as she caught sight of his target, a large snake, poised and ready to strike, not more than ten feet from him. The gunshot was deafening, reverberating in the air as the snake fell to the ground in a macabre fashion.

"Is it . . . dead?" Michelle asked breathlessly.

Gator swung his head in her direction and saw the horrified look on her face. He walked over and kicked the snake with the toe of his boot. "Yeah, I'd say so." He picked it up by the tail. "He's fairly big. I'd say he was the grandaddy of the bunch."

"W-what kind of snake is it?" She realized suddenly that she was trembling.

"Cottonmouth. I'm surprised we didn't run into one sooner."

She glanced around anxiously, scanning the

grass for others. "You think there are more around here?"

"It wouldn't surprise me." At her frightened look, he added, "But don't worry, they're just as scared of us as we are of them. Most of the time they'll run in the opposite direction if they hear you coming. I think I surprised this one." He slung the snake in the water and it landed with a plop, sending ripples in every direction. Michelle shuddered.

"Can we leave now?" she asked, determined to put as much distance as she could between herself and the possibility of more snakes. She was thankful now that Gator's mother had insisted she and Reba spend the night at her place, with its wide, fern-filled front porch and wicker rockers. It seemed a bit more civilized than Reba's cabin or Gator's houseboat. Not only that, but Mrs. Landry had promised to fill her bathtub with warm water so Michelle could take a real bath when she returned. The prospect of that luxury had been on Michelle's mind all day.

"Sure, hop in," he said, motioning her over. He held the boat still while she climbed in. Once she'd settled herself in the bow, he cast the lines and started the motor. A minute later they were on their way. Michelle leaned back and closed her eyes, enjoying the light breeze on her face. It felt good to rest after a long day of hard work.

They hadn't gone more than a hundred feet from the dock before the motor started sputtering. They both glanced up in surprise, but before they could say anything, it died.

Michelle straightened in her seat. "What's wrong? Are we out of gas?"

Gator shook his head. "I just changed gas tanks. Maybe it didn't have time to get gas to the motor." He shrugged. "It's been awhile since I've worked on boats."

"What are we going to do?"

Gator wasn't listening. He'd already moved to the back of the boat, testing hoses, looking into the red gas tank, sniffing it. Finally, he raised up. "I think there's water in the gas line. I can't think of anything else it could be."

"Is it serious?"

"No, but I'll have to clean the gas lines."

"How long will it take?"

"Shouldn't take more than an hour, but that's not our problem."

"Then what is our problem?" she asked, almost dreading his answer.

"We don't have any gas. This was my last tank. It's full, but it won't do us a bit of good if it's got water in it."

"Can't you radio for help?"

"We're too far out."

"Well, don't worry, Reba and your mother will send someone out here for us," she said hopefully.

"I wouldn't count on it."

"Why?"

"Because folks don't like coming way out here on the bayou at night. For one thing, the bayou is always changing and rearranging itself, especially after a storm. A person could get lost and never be found out here."

"Then they'll just have to take the road, for heaven's sake. I know it's much farther that way, but—" She stopped speaking when Gator glanced away. "What's wrong? Did something happen to the road?"

Gator didn't answer right away. "One of the bridges was washed out by the storm." He heard her gasp and looked up. "I didn't want to tell you, because I knew you'd get upset, what with your car still buried under that tree and all. I figured it would only be a couple of days before it was fixed, and I didn't want to bother you with it."

"Oh, well, that's just dandy," she said, feeling her chest swell with anger. "You knew all this time and didn't bother to tell me."

"What good would it have done?"

"I could have . . . maybe made arrangements to have someone drive down from Baton Rouge to get me. I just thought it was a matter of having a tree pulled from my car."

"I hope you don't expect Dr. Kildare to leave his pregnant wife to come down and rescue you," he said dryly.

"Keep Jeffrey out of this."

"Why should I? He's the reason you're so anxious to get back."

"I happen to have a job and responsibilities waiting for me there," she said hotly. "Not that you have any idea what the word 'responsibility' means."

"Here we go again."

"Just look at you. Some sheriff you are. Why, you don't even bother to wear a shirt most of the time."

"That's because I know you prefer me this way."

Anger surged through her body at the smug look he shot her. "Only in your dreams, mister."

Gator reached for the oars.

"What are you doing?"

"I'm going to beat you with this paddle," he said matter-of-factly, "if you don't stop ranting and raving at me like some lunatic. While you've been throwing your temper tantrum, we've drifted farther from the house."

Michelle crossed her arms over her breasts and pressed her lips together in a firm line. She was too angry to speak at the moment.

Thirty minutes later, an arm-weary Gator docked the boat at Reba's backyard once more. Michelle hadn't so much as uttered a word to him in that time, and she clambered out of the boat before he had a chance to put the oars away and assist. She stalked up to the house and slammed inside, wishing the bayou would open up and swallow Gator whole so that she never had to look at him again.

Five

Michelle busied herself inside for the next couple of hours, trying to make use of what light was left for the day. Gator came in once looking for rubbing alcohol, which he planned to use to flush out the fuel line, and once she found it for him, he thanked her abruptly and left. Her mood was so bleak, she decided it was best to say nothing.

Gator glanced at the house from time to time as he worked, but Michelle hadn't budged from the place. He thought about walking to Reba's nearest neighbor, several miles away, but he knew he'd be wasting his time, since that very neighbor was probably still sitting in one of the shelters in town. Besides, he and Michelle were no worse off than the rest of the town at the moment.

Gator knew his mother would not grow concerned right away. He had told her they might drop by City Hall before returning, so she wouldn't expect them back anytime soon. He knew his mother trusted him in the bayou—he certainly knew the dangers—and probably wouldn't start worrying until it got late. He'd lived by his wits for so long that she no longer questioned him. But then his mother had always given him his space, even in his rebellious days when everything he did sent his father into a frenzy.

Gator frowned. His father had never given an inch. Perhaps that's why his mother had gone out of her way to let him make his own decisions, given him the space he so desperately craved. His father had expected him to be a man at ten years old, when he'd watched his house burn to the ground with everything in it—his Hardy Boys mysteries, all the treasures he'd accumulated in his short life. His mother had allowed him to cry against her shoulder. And while his father had ruled with an iron fist, his mother had raised him with love. He had not grieved when his father had died, and he had no desire to grow up like him, this man who literally was worshipped by those he served while his family barely tolerated him. Not once had he ever heard his father tell his mother he loved her. She had cleaned and cooked for him, but he'd never seemed to appreciate it. And he'd never told Gator he loved him, not even as he lay dying of his second heart attack. Remaining true to form, his last words were nothing more than an order, a demand for another pillow beneath his head.

Gator finished cleaning the hose and set it aside. His mood was dark, he knew, but thinking of the man who'd raised him always put him out of sorts for a while. Not that he hadn't long ago come to terms with his feelings about his father. His mother had once told him that his father was not capable of showing love the way most people did, that he expressed love by providing for his family and seeing that his son was properly clothed and schooled. In his father's mind, she explained, that's where his obligation stopped. Gator had decided long ago that if he ever had children, he would not hold back his affection.

But none of that was important right now, he reminded himself. Besides, it was unlikely that he would marry and have children at this point in his life, with all he wanted to see and do. What mattered to him at the moment was getting Michelle and himself back to town. He felt helpless. For someone who was accustomed to being in control, it was not a comfortable feeling. But the damn hurricane had fouled up everything!

Michelle had counted on him to get her back, and he'd let her down. She had every right to be angry. Her entire life was waiting for her back in Baton Rouge, but she was spinning her wheels in the boonies simply because of him. He should have thought to bring another gas tank. He should have checked the progress on the bridge. He should have insisted someone pull that damn tree off her car. But he hadn't, simply because he didn't want to see her go. Once again, he was proving to be a selfish bastard. He promised himself he would do something about it as soon as he reached town, even if he had to repair the bridge with his own bare hands, even if it meant driving Michelle back to Baton Rouge personally and delivering her safely into Dr. Kildare's arms!

Michelle stood in the living room gazing out the window at Gator, who had not budged from his place in the boat for almost two hours. She could barely make him out in the diminishing light, but he looked deep in thought as he stared out at the water. What could he be thinking? she wondered. Guilt stabbed her. She'd had no right to say the things she had to him. From the very beginning, he'd done everything he could for Reba and her, even risked his life to remain with them when the hurricane had hit, instead of taking shelter in City Hall, where it was safer. He'd opened his own home to them, slept on the couch so they could have his bed, and not once had he complained. He'd gone out of his way once again by cleaning up Reba's place, and look what she'd given him in return.

Michelle almost hated herself at the moment. How could she have said all those things after what he'd done for her? She crossed the room, took a deep breath at the back door, and pushed it open.

If Gator heard her walk up, he didn't give any indication. Instead, he merely stared at the gently moving bayou, as though it held some great secret. Michelle picked her way cautiously across the grass, her eyes scanning the area for long, slithery creatures. She stopped at the water's edge.

"I made dinner," she said, her voice hopeful. A light breeze ruffled her hair, and she pushed aside a few strands. "Tuna fish and pork and beans," she added, "which I believe are favorites of yours."

Gator swung his head around slowly. The smile he offered was faint. "I don't believe I've ever had tuna fish and pork and beans."

She nodded. "And if you're lucky, you won't ever have to eat it again after tonight."

He chuckled and turned away.

She sighed heavily, clasping her hands in front of her. "Gator, I feel crummy about the things I said to you. I'm sorry." She blinked when tears stung her eyes. "I know I haven't been easy to get along with. I don't know what's gotten into me except . . . well, I'm tired of eating canned food and washing out of a sink. There's not much I wouldn't do for a hot bubble bath and a bottle of makeup. I never thought of myself as a vain person until this happened, but—" She paused. "Well, it's not important *why* I've been acting like a first-rate jackass." She smiled. "You know, Gator, you always did bring out the worst in me."

When Gator faced her again, he was grinning. He hadn't expected the apology, but he appreciated it just the same. If he had ever bothered to know the inner workings of a woman's mind, he thought to himself, he would have suspected what was bothering her. How utterly female of her to crave a bubble bath when the whole world was turned upside down around them. But he liked that about her. And to be fair, he had to admit she had done more than her share of work. She deserved a bubble bath, dammit!

"So what exactly would you do for a bubble bath, Mic?"

She laughed. He was back to his old self again,

thank goodness. She only hoped they could stay on friendly terms until help came.

Gator did not come in for dinner right away, so Michelle dined alone as the night ate away the rest of the light and deepened the shadows inside the house. She gazed at the flickering candle on the table, feeling a hypnotic pull toward the golden flame. She felt hot and gritty and tired—too tired to go see what Gator was doing. Now and then she caught glimpses of his flashlight through the window, and she wondered what he was up to.

When Gator finally entered the house sometime later, he found Michelle dozing on the couch. For a moment, all he could do was stare at the fetching picture she presented, her hair falling softly across her face, one hand tucked beneath her cheek. Her shorts gave him an unobstructed view of the loveliest legs he'd ever seen—trim ankles, shapely calves and thighs. Her blouse had worked its way up her rib cage again, exposing a wide band of silky-looking skin. Something stirred in his body, and he realized he'd become aroused simply by watching her sleep.

He went about his work, stopping briefly to munch on tuna fish and crackers. Lord, what he'd give for a nice juicy steak with all the trimmings!

Michelle opened her eyes minutes later as he stepped through the back door with a bucket of steaming water.

"You ready for that bubble bath, sleepyhead?" he said, then disappeared into the bathroom before she could answer.

Michelle blinked and raised up slowly, rubbing her eyes. Did he say bubble bath? Surely she'd misunderstood. She padded barefoot across the plank floor, stopping just outside the bathroom door.

Gator emerged wearing a smile. "You're all set, kiddo. I couldn't find bubble bath, so I used dish detergent instead."

Michelle stepped past him and made her way inside the old-fashioned bathroom, where a large decorative candle placed on the side of the tub provided a cozy light. The tub was half-filled with water. She touched it tentatively. "It's hot," she said in disbelief. "Where'd you get all this hot water?"

"I found a big iron pot in one of the sheds," he said, "and heated it over a camp fire. You'd better get in while it's hot. Also"—he handed her a bottle of shampoo—"I thought you could use this. Call me after you wash your hair, and I'll rinse it for you with a bucket of water." He reached for Reba's bathrobe, which was hanging on the back of the bathroom door. "You can put this on and lean over the sink."

After having to do without so many luxuries the past few days, the simple pleasure of a mere bath was more than Michelle had hoped for. "I don't know what to say," she confessed. "Thank you, Gator."

"Just don't let the water out when you're finished," he said. "I want to get in after you."

"You should go first," she said. "After all, you're the one who heated the water and carried it in."

He grinned. "You really want me to?"

She laughed. "No, but I thought it was darn nice of me to suggest it."

His grin broadened. "Call me when you want me to rinse your hair, Mic." He disappeared, closing the bathroom door behind him.

Michelle stepped out of her clothes eagerly and left them in a neat pile on the bathroom floor. She sank into the bathwater a moment later, filling the room with sighs of pleasure. At first she just lay there, letting the water soak into her gritty flesh and soothe her tired muscles. Gator Landry had outdone himself this time, she decided. She took great pleasure soaping herself all over, then rinsed, feeling her skin tingle in response. Finally, she wet her hair and worked up a lather. Once she'd scrubbed her head thoroughly, Michelle piled the long soapy strands on top of her head and stepped out of the tub. She dried herself briskly, mopping her face and neck where the shampoo trickled down, and put on Reba's robe.

Gator came into the bathroom as soon as she called, carrying another bucket of steaming water. He smiled at the sight of her in Reba's robe, a towel draped around her neck. Her skin glowed a healthy color. "Ready to rinse, ma'am?" he asked, testing the water in the bucket to make sure it wasn't too hot.

"Yes sir," she replied, leaning over the old pedestal sink. Gator poured the water over her head slowly and watched the shampoo bubbles wash down the drain. Although it took several buckets of water to rinse her long hair, Gator did not mind in the least. There was something very intimate about washing a woman's hair, he decided, and he liked it. The back of her neck was long and white and sprinkled with downy blond hairs that beckoned a man's lips. He tried to push the thought aside and concentrate on rinsing her golden mane. Afterward, Michelle dried it with a towel and let it fall wet against her shoulders. He wondered if she had any idea how sexy she looked, how sweet she smelled.

"This is the nicest thing anybody has ever done for me," she said, touching his arm gently.

Gator swallowed. It was hell trying to think when she touched him like that or looked at him with her eyes all soft and green. "You didn't stay in very long," he said, his voice sounding strange to his own ears. "I figured you'd be in here awhile."

"I didn't want the water to get cold. If you like, I can try to find something of my grandfather's for you to wear after your bath."

"Yeah, thanks." He handed her the flashlight and moved away quickly, wanting to put some distance between them. The bathroom was too small for the two of them, he decided, with not nearly enough air to breathe. That explained his breathlessness, his light-headedness. Hearing her walk away, he knew immediate relief and almost sighed openly. His heart skittered to a halt when she paused at the door. Their gazes met and locked. It was the longest three seconds of his life. "Anything wrong, Mic?" he said.

She smiled and shook her head, then closed the door behind her. She stood there for a moment, clutching her stomach. It fluttered wildly, as though a flock of wild birds had just taken flight inside her. Her heart pounded, and her knees trembled. Wasn't it just like Gator Landry to do these things to her, she told herself. Just when she felt as if she were in control of things, he had to go and shake her up again.

Michelle hurried upstairs to the guest room, where she knew Reba kept her grandfather's old clothes. She found the man's old velour bathrobe right away and draped it on the bathroom door-knob. She hesitated at the door, listening to the sounds of Gator washing. Her mind was instantly filled with images of him sitting in the tub, his naked body slick and wet, the light from the candle illuminating those black eyes.

Gator emerged sometime later wearing the bathrobe and looking refreshed. Michelle thought he'd never looked sexier. The robe was short on him, the hem falling well above his knees, exposing a pair of hair-roughened calves and thighs that were lean but slightly muscular. She felt her stomach tighten at the sight of him. His wet hair fell about his head carelessly.

"Well, that certainly felt good," he announced, sinking on the couch beside her. The cushion dipped under the weight of his body. He leaned back and propped his feet on Reba's coffee table.

He smelled of soap and male flesh, Michelle noted, kicking her own feet up next to his, trying her darnedest to appear casual about the whole thing. But how could she hope to pull it off when her thoughts refused to cooperate? How was she supposed to forget that he was completely naked beneath that robe?

A large calico cat leaped into her lap and curled into a fat ball. For a moment Michelle and Gator merely sat there, both of them gazing at the candle near their feet.

"When do you think someone will come for us?" she finally asked.

"In the morning probably."

"So we'll sleep here tonight?"

He nodded. "I don't know too many people who'll venture out on the bayou at night."

"I hope Reba isn't worried."

"She knows I'll take care of you, Mic," he said gently.

Michelle raised her green eyes to his black ones. She knew he spoke the truth. Reba might be concerned when she didn't return, but would feel comfortable knowing Gator was with her. And the odd thing about it was Michelle felt equally comfortable. Gator, in his own way, inspired confidence. He might make her mad as the devil sometimes, but she knew she was safe in his care. She smiled at the thought.

Gator didn't miss it. "What're you thinking, Mic?" he asked softly.

"I was just wondering how on earth you came up with a nickname like Gator." Actually, she was trying to come up with something to take her mind off his nearness and the fact that he was stark naked under the robe. It wasn't an easy task, she decided, then wondered if she was turning into some kind of sex maniac.

He chuckled. "How do you know that's not my real name?"

"Reba told me your real name was Matthieu."

He arched one dark brow. "So you were asking Reba about me?"

She blushed. "No. Reba mentioned it the day of the storm." She shot him a sideways glance. "So how'd you get the name?"

He shrugged. "I once raised a baby alligator from birth. The kids called me Alligator Man for a while, then just shortened it to Gator. I never cared much for my real name anyway."

"I like it."

He turned to her. "You do? Well, that's a first. You finally discovered something about me you like."

His words surprised her. "I've always liked you, Gator," she said. "I just don't understand you, that's all. You're so . . . different from the other men I know."

He faced her, propping his elbow on the back of the couch. Michelle tensed when his robe fell open slightly, exposing part of his chest. He didn't seem to notice.

Gator studied her in the flickering candlelight. It accentuated the lovely contours of her face, bringing out her high cheekbones and emphasizing her wide green eyes. She had never looked lovelier. "Is that so bad? To be different from other people?"

Michelle took a long time answering, not only because it was difficult concentrating with him so close, but because she felt her answer was important. Maybe it would explain to both of them why their relationship was so tense. "Not bad, I guess. I just feel . . . unsure about myself when I'm with you. I never know what to expect from you." And she never knew what to expect from herself, she wanted to add.

"And you don't like surprises, huh?" He smiled gently.

"I like to know where I stand with a person."

He pondered her remark. "Well, you've always been way up there on top as far as I'm concerned, Mic." He reached for a lock of damp hair and rubbed it between his fingers. She didn't seem to mind. "The other girls never came close to you."

"But you didn't let it stop you from giving them a tumble just the same, did you?" she asked, offering him a wry smile.

"I never had any reason not to." He wound the lock of hair around his index finger. "I never forgot you, Mic," he said simply and honestly.

"But I had no way of knowing that, did I?"

"What were we going to do at fifteen?"

"Fifteen years have passed, Gator. That's a long time." She was surprised by her own words.

He released her hair and let his hand fall to her shoulder. "Mic, if I had thought for one minute you were interested in hearing from me—" He didn't finish the sentence.

"I thought you'd at least write."

"I wanted to, believe me."

"But you didn't."

"I was scared."

"You, scared?" She looked doubtful. "I can't believe Gator Landry would be scared of anything."

His eyes held hers tight. "I'm scared to death right now, Mic." At her look of surprise, he went on. "I'm scared about all these feelings that come to the surface when I look at you. I'm scared because of the things I want to say to you, of the things I want to do to you."

His words sucked the breath right out of her. "What . . . things?"

"Things like—" He hesitated. "Like maybe I fell in love with you that summer," he finally said. "I know I was young at the time, but I think I loved you just the same. Sometimes you just know these things. You know when a person has touched you in a way that nobody else ever came close to doing. And those feelings never went away. They grew and intensified over the years." He raised a finger to her neck and stroked the white skin there, finding it incredibly soft. "I must've made love to you a million times in my dreams, Mic," he confessed.

Michelle shivered at the sound of his voice, her skin prickled as his fingers trickled up her neck and traced the shell of her ear. She attempted to smile, but she could feel her bottom lip tremble with the effort. "And did you . . . enjoy it?"

"More than you'll ever know."

For a moment, all they could do was stare at each other. Michelle knew he was going to kiss her, and she couldn't have moved if she'd wanted to. His gaze held her rooted to the spot. He lowered his face to hers slowly and hesitated one heart-stopping moment before touching his lips to hers.

She had been waiting for him to kiss her, Michelle realized. She raised her lips eagerly to his, and when his tongue prodded her lips open, she was only too happy to oblige. She met the thrust of his tongue boldly, and the kiss deepened and became more erotic than anything she'd ever experienced. He sampled the textures of her mouth, sliding his tongue across her teeth and dipping into the dark nooks and crannies as though seeking a hidden treasure. He took her bottom lip between his teeth and tugged it gently, then raised his calloused palms to her face and turned her head just so, giving him free access to her mouth. Michelle had never been so thoroughly kissed in her life.

The kiss went on, Gator pausing only briefly so they could gulp air into their lungs. Their lips clung together hungrily, melding as one. Gator's body was on fire, his muscles rigid in an attempt to hold himself in check. He was so hard for her he hurt. When he finally raised his head, they were both gasping. Her lips were damp and swollen, and he had a sudden brief picture of those same lips on his body. When he spoke, his voice was raw with need. "If you're going to stop me, do it now, Mic, because in another three seconds you won't be able to. I've never taken a woman against her will, but this thing is out of control."

Michelle was almost frightened by the intensity of his gaze. "Gator, I can't think—"

"The time for thinking is over, Mic," he said gruffly. "You either want me or you don't." He gazed at her for a moment, feeling more vulnerable than he ever had in his life. He was almost crazy from wanting her, but he wasn't about to make the first move. This was what fifteen years of dreaming over her had done to him, he thought. It was scary to want a woman that much.

Michelle slipped her arms around his neck and pulled him close, so close his lips brushed hers as lightly as a butterfly's wing. Heat radiated from his body. "I do want you, Gator," she whispered against his mouth. "I've always wanted you."

Six

Gator gazed at her for several seconds as the full measure of her words sank in. Her eyes were soft with invitation, her slight smile beguiling and sexy as all get-out. He leaned his head forward, touching her nose playfully with his own, the look in his eyes saying more than he possibly could at the moment. He reached for the large ornamental candle he'd carried from the bathroom and handed it to her, surprised to find himself trembling. Then, without wasting any more time, he stood and scooped her up high into his arms.

Gator almost groaned out loud when the tops of his arms made contact with her bare thighs and hips. Lord, had he known she wasn't wearing anything under that old bathrobe, he would have lost control a long time ago. But then he remembered that she always washed her panties out in the bathroom sink at night and hid them under her bath towel. He would never have guessed as much, had he not grabbed her towel by accident one morning to dry his face and ended up with that wisp of silk in his hands. He grinned now, remembering how his gut had tightened at the sight of those pale blue panties edged with fragile ivory lace, and how he hadn't been able to think straight for the rest of the day.

"What are you smiling at?" Michelle asked, interrupting his train of thought.

His grin broadened. "Wouldn't you like to know."

She clucked her tongue. "You nasty boy." When he pretended to look offended, she laughed. "I know that wicked gleam of yours, Gator Landry. Whatever you're thinking, it has to be bad."

Gator kissed her lightly on the tip of her nose and carried her up the stairs to the guest room, the candle lighting the way. Michelle cupped the flame with her palm to keep it from blowing out. Once he entered the room, Gator set her down gently and took the candle from her. The room was bathed in a golden light that made it appear warm and cozy. Reba's old furniture didn't look as harsh in the soft light; instead, it added character to the room. But Gator couldn't have cared less.

He held the candle, staring at Michelle as though she were an apparition, which wasn't far from the truth as far as he was concerned. If someone had told him a week ago that he'd be sharing her bed, he would have laughed. He still couldn't believe it. Surely he had done something good in his life to deserve this.

"Take off the robe, Mic," he said gently. "I've

waited fifteen years to see you, and I can't stand it any longer." When she hesitated, he added, "Please."

Michelle reached for the tie on her grandmother's robe and pulled the knot free, fixing her gaze on Gator's Adam's apple as she did so—anything to keep from looking into those black eyes. Every insecurity she'd ever had reared its ugly head, but it was too late to worry about that now, she reminded herself. Slowly, she pulled the garment open and let it trail down her arms. She caught it in her hands and held it briefly, then let it drop with a whisper at her feet.

Gator heard his own quick intake of breath as the robe fell away. His gaze greedily devoured the woman before him—the gentle sloping shoulders, the high pear-shaped breasts with dark pink nipples, the sight of which stole his rational thought. Her waist dipped at her navel, then flared into generous but well-proportioned hips. The light brown tuft at her thighs sent a tremor through his body and a rumble of pleasure through his chest. He raised his eyes to her face. Something tugged at his gut as he read the doubt and uncertainty there. She looked so vulnerable at the moment; he didn't quite know what to make of it. He set the candle on the nightstand and regarded her nakedness once again, tightening his fists into balls at his sides to keep from reaching out. He didn't want to rush her, even though his body cried out for her with every breath he drew.

When Gator spoke, his voice was low, bordering on reverent. "It was worth waiting fifteen years,

Mic." Then he took her into his arms. She went willingly.

His mouth was warm and soft, giving way to a kiss that was gentle and caring and blessedly unhurried. Michelle leaned into the embrace, drawing strength from his big body and confidence with each loving caress. She could feel him holding back, taking his time with her, and she appreciated it. His hands felt like toughened leather as he stroked her back and kneaded her thighs.

Soon, the kisses turned hot and frantic, Gator's tongue more insistent. He broke contact and moved his mouth to the hollow of her throat, where her pulse beat wildly. He moved to an earlobe, nipped it gently, then dipped his tongue inside. Michelle shivered.

Gator had cautioned himself against hurrying, wanting to savor each moment and give her time to relax with him, but he could not look at her without touching her. He raised his hands slowly and covered each breast with an open palm. Her skin looked like fine porcelain against his dark hands. Her nipples were the same color as the petals on his mother's prized roses, he noted as he stroked them. Finally, because he couldn't stand it any longer, he lowered his head and took one nipple into his mouth. He kissed and suckled and tugged it gently between his lips, and smiled when the nipple budded.

Michelle raised her hands to his head and slipped her fingers through his unruly black hair, holding his face close as his lips paid homage to each breast. For a moment, she merely held him there, stroking his head as a feeling of tenderness washed over her. The feeling was alien to her, almost maternal, and she wondered at it. But then slowly this feeling was replaced with something more intense and erotic, warming her lower belly and spiraling upward and outward until her limbs literally tingled. The warm mushy feeling in her stomach turned hot and congregated at the juncture of her thighs, making her feel incredible pleasure and anticipation all at once. And then he shrugged out of his own robe.

Michelle gazed at Gator with sheer feminine appreciation. There wasn't an ounce of fat on the man, only bronzed flesh and hard sinew. She touched his chest lightly, running her hands through the springy curls that grasped her fingers like silken rings. She trailed one hand over his stomach, feeling the muscle flex beneath her touch.

"Touch me, Mic," he said simply. Michelle complied, lowering her hand to where the black hair grew dense.

Gator squeezed his eyes shut as she gently closed her palm around him. How many times had he felt her do just that in his dreams? he wondered. His blood roared in his ears as she began a gentle lover's caress that in just a matter of seconds had him hard and ready for her. "Not yet, Mic," he said, stilling her small hand in his. He raised the hand to his face and kissed her open palm.

Taking her into his arms once more, Gator eased Michelle onto the bed and laid her down gently, following as she went, the mattress dipping under their weight. Once again, he moved his mouth to her breasts, then inched his way to her navel, swirling his tongue around her belly button. Then he kissed his way to her concave stomach. His hands never quieted, stroking and tantalizing her flesh. Finally, he probed the curls between her thighs and dipped his fingers inside. He grinned when he found what he wanted. She was moist.

"Oh, baby," he moaned. His black eyes glittered in the candlelight.

Michelle sighed with ultimate pleasure as Gator's fingers made contact with the very root of her desire. She arched against his hand, letting her thighs fall to the side as he worked his magic. And even as her inhibitions tried to keep her from losing control, Gator whispered words of encouragement—some of them sweet and tender, others erotic enough to bring a rosy blush to her cheeks and send her over the edge. She shuddered as a feeling of absolute delight shimmied up her body.

His mouth followed the same route, his breath hot on her thighs, his tongue so light, she thought she was imagining it. She pulled him closer. Gator grinned and raised his head, and she whimpered her objection.

"Throw your legs over my shoulders, darlin'," he said.

Michelle did as she was told. His mouth returned, urgent, allowing his tongue to alternately probe deeply inside her and flick lightly across her sensitive bud. His hands never stilled, stroking and kneading her body, lifting her so he could partake of all her offerings. Michelle was both shocked and delighted. Nothing was off-limits to Gator Landry. There were no out-of-bounds, sacred areas. All was his for the taking, and to hell with propriety.

Michelle writhed and squirmed under his masterful ministrations. There was no escaping.

Gator breathed the very essence of her and knew that he could live to be an old man and never forget her erotic scent. It would follow him through eternity, just as those green eyes would, and the sound of her voice.

Finally heat surged through her, down her thighs and loins, and exploded like thunder in a white-hot flash that held her in its grip for several wonderful, maddening seconds. Gator matched her tempo, her frenzied movement, welcoming the tumult that quaked her body and left her trembling.

Through heavy-lidded eyes, Michelle watched Gator move over her, thinking he had never looked more desirable and sexy. He paused briefly at the base of her thighs, then he entered her with one fluid thrust that lifted her hips from the bed.

For a moment, Gator merely lay there, his body propped on his elbows. He gazed down at Michelle and thought she had never looked lovelier, her green eyes soft, her smile tender. He kissed her lightly on the lips and very slowly began to move inside her. She was hot and tight, her flesh gripping him so sensuously he couldn't think straight. There wasn't a hair on his body that wasn't totally sensitized to the woman beneath him, and he wondered if a man could feel so good and live to tell it. He kissed her again, deeply, and her tongue met his eagerly, just as her hips met his steady thrusts. They moved in unison, as though in time to the same dance tune, hard lines complementing soft curves. He heard her breath quicken, and he knew his control was slipping with every heartbeat. She cried out his name and arched against him, just as she had only moments before when he'd sipped from her body. Control was lost. He gave one finale thrust, hovered on the brink, then shuddered.

When Gator finally raised his head from her shoulder, he was smiling. Actually, he was grinning from ear to ear, as though over some private joke.

Michelle blushed as rational thought returned, bringing with it a hefty dose of guilt. She eyed him cautiously. "What's so funny?"

Gator didn't answer right away. Instead, he rolled aside and gathered her into his arms. He sighed, and the sound was one of pure male satisfaction. "I was just thinking how damn good we are together," he said. After a moment, he frowned. "Too bad we let all those years pass us by before we did anything about it." He sighed again, this time wistfully. "All that good lovin' we missed out on. Kind of makes you sad, doesn't it?" He stroked the back of her neck while he talked.

His words filled her with a sense of dread. How like Gator to be so casual about what had just happened between them, when for her, the earth had literally moved. And wasn't it just like Gator to make love to her more intimately than she'd ever been made love to in her life and act as though it were no big deal. He'd simply referred to it as a bit of "good lovin'." Her gazes fluttered up Gator's chest to his face. She still felt a bit shy toward him after what they'd shared, but he was watching her as though expecting some sort of a reply.

"I think lovemaking is highly overrated in a relationship, Gator," she said. "It's important, but it's not *that* important." There now. She could be just as casual about it as the next person.

Gator knew a moment of intense disappointment. But what could he expect? he asked himself. Just because their lovemaking was the greatest thing that had ever happened to him didn't mean it had been the same for her. "Well, you certainly seemed to be taking it seriously a moment ago," he muttered.

Michelle's face flamed. Wasn't it just like Gator Landry to poke fun at her. Why had she thought their lovemaking would alter him, anyway? She pulled away, but he refused to let her go. Instead, he laughed and pulled her tighter against him.

"I'm just teasing you, honey," he said. "I like a passionate woman. In fact, I prefer it." That wasn't entirely true, he reminded himself. He wanted her to tell him she wasn't normally so passionate, that *he* had been the reason for that passion, that he had done and made her feel things no other man had ever come close to making her feel.

"You're laughing at me, Gator. You're always laughing at me."

He was clearly surprised by her outburst. "I'm not laughing at you, honey. I was just teasing. There's nothing wrong with having a little fun in bed, is there?"

"You're always laughing at me," she repeated, "wearing that grin . . . that cocky smile . . . as though you have something on me. You're doing it right now, Gator Landry," she said, pointing an accusing finger at him. "It makes me so self-conscious, I can't think straight. I wonder if I have spinach between my teeth or if the back of my neck is dirty."

"Gee, Mic, I didn't realize—" He paused and his look sobered. "I don't do it on purpose. I'll admit I sometimes lose my train of thought when I'm with you, and my mind sort of goes off in another direction. Sometimes my thoughts get a little X-rated, I reckon. Maybe that's what makes me smile." He shrugged. "I'm not trying to give you a complex. I just can't think straight when you're around. You make me edgy."

"*I* make *you* edgy?" she echoed in disbelief.

He nodded. "Hell yeah, you make me edgy. Here I am trying to concentrate on getting this town put back together, and you're flittin' around in those tight shorts of yours and that blouse that shows your cute little belly button every time you raise your arms. How'm I suppose to get any work done, for Pete's sake?"

For a moment, she merely stared at him. It was nice to believe she tempted him just a little. And it was flattering to know she could make Gator Landry want her after all these years. It gave her a feeling of confidence that she hadn't known in

FREE BOOK OFFER!

a long time. Michelle smiled. She felt beautiful and seductive. She raised her hand to Gator's magnificent chest. "So I'm a distraction to you, huh?" she teased.

"You might say that. And it's annoying as hell sometimes. It's sort of like having an itch you can't reach." He shot her a devilish grin and captured her hand with his. He squeezed it once and raised it to his face then kissed her palm. She thought lovemaking was overrated, did she? Well, he would show her just how important healthy sex was between a man and a woman. He would make love to her till her toes curled, until her hair stood on end. And when he was finished with her, she would know she'd been made love to by Gator Landry.

Gator moved her hand over him. "But somebody has to put up with it, so it might as well be me."

Their lovemaking was slow and leisurely, and when Gator pulled Michelle on top of him, he filled her completely, loving the way she fit around him so tightly. He moved against her slowly, torturing her—every time she came close to climax, he went completely still. Finally, she cried out, pleading with him not to stop. And, though he'd wanted to teach her a lesson, his heart was tugged by the vulnerable look in her eyes. He gave her what she wanted, thrusting into her with a vengeance that surprised even him. She would not forget him soon, he promised her silently. By the time his groan of pleasure drifted upward, she was totally spent.

Afterward, he kissed her deeply, unable to tear

his lips away from hers. He thought it odd because he'd never been much for kissing, other than the few obligatory kisses before and after sex. But he wanted to kiss Michelle, he realized. In fact, he enjoyed it immensely.

They talked late into the night and fell asleep in each other's arms.

Seven

When Gator opened his eyes the following morning, he found Michelle watching him from her pillow. He smiled and stretched, then reached for her and pulled her into his arms. "G'morning, beautiful. How'd you sleep?"

"We have to talk."

Gator blinked at the seriousness of her voice. "Is something wrong?"

"Something is very wrong," she said. "We didn't practice safe sex last night."

He blinked again. "You mean you might be pregnant?"

She rolled her eyes and raised up. "Of course not. But we didn't do anything to prevent . . . well . . . you know."

He shook his head, looking suddenly amused. "No, I don't know. You tell me."

"We could have passed something on. A disease. Neither of us was protected."

The smile faded as he sat up. "Oh, I get it. You're afraid I gave you something, right?" He was surprised how much the idea stung. He swung his legs off the bed and stood, planting a hand on one out-thrust hip as though totally unaware of his nakedness. Michelle thought he had never looked more magnificent, with the early-morning light bathing his skin. "I'll bet you didn't stop and ask Dr. Kildare if he was free from cooties before you let *him* make love with you."

"You're wrong about that."

He ignored her comment. Damn, but she knew how to get the morning off to a bad start. He felt as if she'd just poured ice water over his head. "But I'm not a hotshot doctor, so I'm not good enough for you, right? I'm okay for cleaning up your grandmother's property and running you all over town in my truck, but I'm just a little too nasty to bring into the house. Is that about the way it is, Mic?" For the first time Gator realized he was shouting, and he lowered his voice. "You don't have anything to worry about, princess. I'm clean." He grabbed his robe and slammed out of the room, literally shaking the house.

Michelle followed, her chest filling with anger. She threw open the bedroom door and ran to the top of the stairs. "Gator Landry, don't you just walk out on me and slam the door in my face. Who do you think you are!"

Gator paused near the middle of the stairs. He turned around slowly and made his way back up, his head hitched high, his black eyes cool. "Who do you think *you* are?"

"I'm a grown woman," she said, "who usually

gives more thought to simply falling into bed with a man. But last night—" She paused. "I don't know what got into me. I wasn't thinking." He didn't understand. She could see that he was offended. "I've traveled all over the state with other nurses speaking to young men and women about using caution where sex is concerned. I keep a supply of condoms in my purse at all times."

He looked surprised. "You keep rubbers in your purse?"

"I certainly do. It's a habit I suggest other women pick up as well."

He cocked his head to the side and regarded her. "How long does it take you to go through a box of, say, twelve?" He wasn't sure he felt comfortable with the thought that she was always prepared for sex.

"That's not important."

He arched one brow. "It is to me."

"The point is I'm always protected. It may take me the rest of my life to finish off this box, but at least it's there if I need it. I can't afford to take risks, and neither can you."

Some of his anger abated when he realized she wasn't attacking him personally. Not that he blamed her, of course. His reputation wasn't the best. And in this day and age, she had every right to be cautious. He shouldn't have blown his stack so quickly. Gator climbed the stairs slowly and paused one step below her. She had thrown on her robe carelessly, without tying it. He let his eyes take in the vertical slit of skin that peeked through.

"I usually do protect myself, Mic," he finally said. "I just didn't feel I had to with you." His eyes locked with hers. "You're safe with me, honey, I promise. I wouldn't let you put yourself at risk, believe me. No matter how much I wanted you."

For some reason, she did believe him. Gator Landry might have his faults, but she could not imagine him taking chances with her health or life. "I'm sorry I had to bring it up."

He fingered the tie on her robe. "You were right to," he said. "I shouldn't have gotten so riled up over it." He paused and smiled. "You think maybe I could borrow from your stash?" he asked, his eyes full of mischief. "I seem to be short at the moment. Unless, of course, you've used them all."

She slapped him playfully. "It's a brand-new box, silly. I haven't even used the first."

"Mind if I ask how long you've had that box?"

She regarded him. "Why?"

" 'Cause I'm a selfish bastard with double standards, that's why."

She smiled softly. There was something to be said for honesty. "I've had it for almost six months now."

He was pleased with her answer, and it showed. "I didn't have any right to ask."

"I know."

"Why'd you tell me?"

She shrugged. "Because I have nothing to hide. But I would have expected you to accept an alternative answer as well."

He nodded. "I'd like to think I would have accepted it, Mic, but I can't swear to it. I'm jealous and selfish, and I know it. I prefer to think you've been sitting around all these years waiting for me."

"I'd like to think the same of you, Gator, but I know that's not likely."

Gator reached for her, slipping his big hands inside her robe, where she was still warm from sleep. Her long hair was tousled about her head, her eyes still sleep-filled. "I want to make love to you again, Michelle Thurston," he said simply.

She smiled softly. "And I want you to make love to me, Matthieu Landry."

He gazed at her for a moment, liking the way she said his name. It sounded low and sexy on Michelle's lips. He followed her up the stairs and closed the bedroom door behind them.

Reba Kenner and Fiona Landry sat on the cozy, fern-filled front porch and sipped their coffee while Mae West warmed herself in a pool of early-morning sun. Reba drained her coffee cup and set it on the little wicker table nearby.

"You reckon we should send someone after them?"

Fiona shrugged. "No need to rush."

"What if they kill each other? They fight like cats and dogs sometimes."

Fiona laughed. "Michelle's a nurse, isn't she? If either of them gets hurt, she should be able to take care of it."

"What do you think they're doing?"

"Who knows? A man and woman all alone out there in the bayou . . ." She paused, and her face took on a dreamy-eyed expression. "So romantic."

Reba crossed her arms. "It won't be romantic if they find out we put water in that gas tank."

Fiona waved the statement aside. "They won't find out. Besides, we did them a favor. Those two have been crazy about each other for years, but they're too blasted stubborn to do anything about it. We just gave them a gentle nudge. They'll thank us in the end. And one day we'll all look back on it and laugh."

"Does that mean one day you'll tell 'em what we did?"

"No. This secret is going with me to the grave."

"So what time should we send someone after them?"

"Oh, let's give them another hour or so."

Gator removed the sizzling meat from the frying pan and placed it on the plate Michelle held in her hand. "Breakfast is served, ma'am," he announced with a flourish. He then moved the frying pan from his camp fire and put on a pan of water to boil so they could have instant coffee.

Michelle gazed at the fried Spam dully. Oh, what she'd give for a stack of buttermilk pancakes dripping with butter and syrup, and a tall glass of cold milk, she thought. "I'll carry this inside," she said, trying to muster up a little enthusiasm over their meager breakfast. "I found half a loaf of bread in the pantry that's still good."

Gator followed her into the house and to the kitchen, where Michelle had laid out plates and silverware on the small table. He waited for her to sit down, then took the chair across from her.

She forked the meat onto their plates and handed him the package of bread. He took it, but his gaze was trained on her. She'd combed her hair, and it lay against her shoulders like a silky curtain. He still remembered how it had felt between his fingers as he'd rinsed the shampoo from it the night before, how it had felt against his shoulder. After the lovemaking they'd shared, it was impossible for him to look at her without wanting her.

Michelle glanced up from her plate and caught him staring. She smiled. "What are you thinking?"

He shrugged. "I'm thinking how much I'd like to take you to a nice steak restaurant."

"Steak." She said the word reverently. "Do you think we'll ever eat fresh meat and vegetables again?"

He grinned. "One day, Mic."

She sighed wistfully. "Do you think life will ever return to normal after this?"

He met her gaze. "Not for me."

She knew he spoke the truth. They could repair the power lines and get the town back on its feet after the storm, but life would never be the same. In the past few days, especially in the last twelve hours, her life had changed dramatically. No, things would never be normal again.

Michelle took a bite of her sandwich and chewed, but she was uncomfortably aware that Gator was watching her. "What are you going to do when this is over?" she asked. "When things are as normal as they're going to get."

Gator pondered her question. "Well, first I'm going to clean up this one area in town where we have a lot of trouble. I'd already started doing it, but the storm sort of put matters on hold. There's a couple of kids who are real troublemakers and—" He stopped. " 'Course there's not much for a kid to do in this town. You know? We only have one theater, and it plays the same movie for weeks at a time. This place is really hard up for entertainment. It's no surprise the kids get into trouble."

"Don't you have a YMCA?"

"Yeah, but there's not much to it. We don't have the funds."

"You should ask for volunteers. And more money so you can start a youth program," she added. "If the crime rate here among youth has picked up so, then you have every right to go to City Hall and ask for help with the problem. The program I'm involved with is strictly on a volunteer basis. We travel throughout the state and speak on issues concerning young people. Not just diseases, mind you. We speak on alcohol and drugs. We have people speak on the importance of a good education. We've even implemented a program that is similar to Jesse Jackson's PUSH program. And it's all done on a voluntary basis. I could check on the possibility of having your parish included in our tour."

"That's all fine and dandy, Mic, but I don't want the responsibility." At her look of surprise, he went on. "Not that I don't want the best for this town," he said, "but I don't want to be the one to do it. I have other plans for my life."

She nodded. "I know. Have you got someone in mind to take over?"

"There are a couple of good deputies who might be interested. I didn't really have a chance to discuss it with them before the storm hit and everything went to hell around here. Before that, I was mainly concerned about finding out who'd robbed my mother. You see, I had planned to use my badge to get back at them."

"That's only human."

"Yes, but not any reason to take a job you don't want in the first place. I was more interested in revenge at the time, I suppose. But my mother is all I have left in this world."

"How come you never married and had children?" She knew she was being nosy, but couldn't help it. She wanted to know more about the man, *had* to know more. She should have known that sleeping with him would bring out this curious and caring side of her.

"I never had anything to offer a woman. And when I worked the sugar cane fields . . . well, there wasn't room in my life for anything else."

"Tell me about it."

He shrugged. "I was just traveling through when I came upon this place, all run-down. The old man who owned it laughed in my face when I asked for a job. He said he hadn't had a decent crop in years. We were both in bad shape. He couldn't keep good help, and I couldn't find a job 'cause of my bad records with juvenile hall. So I offered to help him out in exchange for room and board. It took a long time to get the place on its feet again. I would have left long before, had I not gotten attached to the old guy. I guess I sort of made him a father figure. In the end, he made me a full partner, and the place made money. Lots of money. I sold out after awhile."

"Do you ever hear from him?"

"He sent me a postcard a couple of weeks ago. I never answered it. I'm not one for writing letters."

"Yes, I know."

Gator smiled. "I might have made an exception if I had known you wanted to hear from me."

Michelle decided it would be safer to talk about something else. "Surely you met someone during that time whom you thought you might want to marry one day," she said.

His gaze locked with hers. "I had my share of women, if that's what you want to know, Mic. But there was no one steady. I think a couple of them got serious, invited me over to meet their family. That's usually when I lost interest and found somebody new. I know that sounds insensitive, but I didn't want to mislead anyone. And now—" He paused and shrugged. "I'm probably getting too old to marry and have a bunch of kids. I've always done exactly what I wanted. A wife probably wouldn't like it."

She nodded. "You're probably right about that."

"Besides, I'd feel like a caged animal. I like my freedom. Not that I would do anything wrong, mind you. Like I said, I never sleep with more than one woman at a time. Less complicated that way. But I don't like having to ask someone's permission before I do something."

"You could always have an open marriage."

"Meaning?"

"Meaning you and your wife have an understanding. You could do what you wanted, and she could do as she pleased."

He leaned forward and grinned. "Who is going to watch our kids?"

"You'll have to take turns. These are modern times we live in, Gator."

He pondered it. "I don't think I'd feel comfortable with my wife out alone at night. You never know what might happen."

"She could go with friends."

"Yeah, but—"

"Don't you trust her?"

"Of course I do. I wouldn't marry her unless I trusted her completely. But that doesn't mean I have to trust the people she's with."

Michelle smiled. "You know what I think? I think you've got a bad case of double standards. You want to have your cake and eat it too, Gator Landry. You're not going to find many women who'd put up with that kind of philosophy."

He arched one brow, and his amusement was clear in his black eyes. "You'd be surprised, Mic. Some women still prefer us macho types."

"Oh, baloney! You're living in prehistoric times, Gator. I suggest you get with the program."

Gator grinned and leaned back in his chair. His expression was cocky. He loved to see her all riled up. Her eyes glittered like cut glass. "What's wrong, Mic, don't they have any real men left where you live?"

She pushed her chair from the table and stood. "A real man doesn't have to live by a perverse set of rules, Gator. He's confident enough about his masculinity not to feel he has to throw his weight around with a woman." She picked up her saucer and carried it to the sink. As far as she was concerned, the conversation was finished.

Gator's chair scraped the floor as he shoved away from the table. Picking up his own saucer, he crossed the room, closing the distance between them. He stood behind her for a moment, his body only inches from hers. She felt him there, he knew. He could tell by the way her back had stiffened, as though she were daring him to get closer. He took another step and reached around her to set the saucer in the sink. She jumped when the plate made contact with the porcelain.

Michelle gritted her teeth as Gator came even closer. She could feel the heat of his body, feel the hairs on the back of her neck rise. She closed her eyes when he pressed himself against her. "What are you doing?" she asked breathlessly. She could hear the laughter in his voice when he spoke, could feel his need pressing into her hips.

"I'm trying to show you how confident I am about my . . . uh, masculinity," he said.

She blushed. "There's more to it than that," she said. "It's a feeling you get inside."

"Turn around, Mic," he said softly. When she didn't budge, he rolled his eyes heavenward. "Please," he added.

Michelle faced him, then wished she hadn't. He was so close, so uncomfortably close, she could see the stubble on his unshaven face. She tried to take a step back, but her hips met the cabinet. Gator placed his hands on the countertop on either side of her, leaning forward slightly, his breath fanning her cheek.

"You make me kind of crazy, Michelle Thurston, you know that? You always have." He pressed his body against hers as he spoke, and her pelvis cradled his fullness. "Every time you're near I get this urge to throw you over my shoulder and whisk you off to my cave. Yes, I said cave," he added with a chuckle. "I guess you bring out the beast in me, huh?" When she didn't speak, he raised a finger to her lips and brushed them gently. "Is that so bad, Mic? To want to have a little control over the woman you're crazy about?"

"A relationship should be fifty-fifty," she said primly.

He grinned. "Is that how they talk at cocktail parties and luncheons these days, honey? All that sounds good, but there are times when a man wants to be in charge. Call it ego, I don't care, but sometimes a man likes to feel as though he has swept the woman off her feet. There's a time and place for flowers and poetry and other niceties, but in bed, a man should be able to do his share of sweating and grunting and—"

"Does this recital have a point," she interrupted, "or are you simply trying to shock me?"

"I have a feeling you haven't been around many men who've shocked or surprised you lately. Maybe it would do you good to get a little raunchy, Mic. Maybe the experience would wipe those worry lines from your forehead." He raised his hand to her hairline and traced the tiny lines over her brow.

"I'm not a prude, Gator," she said, "and I'll be

the first to admit that making love is healthy for a person, both physically and emotionally. But what about the other things involved in a relationship? What about love and trust and friendship? And how can you expect a woman to want you in bed if she feels oppressed outside of the bedroom? Yes, I like for a man to be in control at times, but there are also times I want to be on equal footing."

He frowned. "You want a wimp."

"I don't want a wimp. But I wouldn't sit home while my man is out running around doing God-knows-what. It works both ways, Gator. If you find a woman willing to live with your double standards, odds are she's not worth having."

The smile he gave her was slow and lazy. "You think you've got it all figured out, don't you?"

She leveled her gaze at him, and her own smile was smug. "Let me just say this, Gator Landry: No man of mine would be in a hurry to leave my side."

His smile widened. "Now, that's the kind of talk I like to hear." He stepped closer and slipped his arms around her waist. "You know, I'm beginning to think a man would be crazy to leave you at home alone. You might just be woman enough to pin him down."

She offered him a coy smile. "Yes, but what makes you think there's a man out there who could hold *me* down, Gator Landry?"

Eight

Gator saw the challenge in her green eyes and hitched his chin higher. "I reckon at my age I know how to keep a woman happy, Mic."

"In the bedroom, maybe," she replied evenly, "but people can't stay in bed all day. What have you got to offer a woman outside the sheets, Gator? There are many different sides to a woman, you know. She likes to be charmed and courted. You don't just grab her by the hair and drag her into the bedroom."

"I can charm the socks off a possum at nine hundred yards, lady."

He obviously wasn't taking her seriously. "And when you're finished 'grunting and sweating,' as you call it, a woman wants to be cuddled and sweet-talked and—"

"I can do that."

"For a while, perhaps. But life doesn't consist of candlelight dinners and moonlight swims and necking on the sofa. There's another side to it— the grocery store, the dry cleaner, housework, yard work—"

"You sure know how to cool a man's ardor," he said laughingly.

"It's difficult to be all things to a woman," she said. "Sex is important, but it should be like dessert in a relationship. Everything else has to be good between two people for the sex to be good."

"You make it sound like a job, Mic. That takes all the fun out of it. Why can't two people just enjoy what they have while it lasts?"

"Because the harder you work at it, the more enjoyable it is, and the longer it lasts. Perhaps forever."

"Forever?" He looked skeptical. "That's a long time. I can't think past next week. I don't want my life so neatly planned, Mic. I like surprises." He shoved his hands in his pockets and walked over to a window, looking out at the bayou. A fine mist still clung to the trees and made the vegetation appear greener somehow, more lush and verdant. "I suppose Dr. Kildare met all your criteria, huh?"

Michelle didn't answer right away. "He came close."

He faced her. "And how was dessert?"

Michelle's face turned red. "That's personal."

"This whole conversation is personal, Mic. But you brought it up, and you don't seem to mind exposing my faults. I guess I'm just trying to understand you better. Figure out exactly what you want in a man."

He had no idea why he was going to so much

trouble. He obviously couldn't come close to meeting her standards, and he wasn't sure he wanted to. The mere thought of tying himself down to one woman for the rest of his life made him shudder. And what about all those domestic chores she'd mentioned? Why buy groceries when you could eat out? His groceries consisted of the bare necessities: beer, pretzels, and chocolate milk. And a man didn't have to mess with yard work when he lived on a houseboat.

Michelle was still pondering his question. She sighed. "Dessert with Jeffrey was like . . . apple pie, I suppose. Tasty but wholesome."

"Wholesome?" He repeated the word silently and grinned. A million questions sprang to mind, but he didn't voice them. He had no right. Instead, he thrust one hip to the side and cocked his head. "So what was it like with me, Mic? Dessert, that is."

She shook her head. He really was a smug son of a gun, she thought. "You know it was good."

Male ego prodded him on. "But what would you compare it to?"

She wished now she'd never said anything. But Gator wouldn't give up until she told him. "Well, with you it's more like . . ." She paused and smiled and blushed again. "A hot fudge sundae with all the trimmings."

"Is that good?"

"Of course it's good. You have the hot fudge on one hand, nice and warm and gooey. Then there's the shivery-cold ice cream, the crunchiness of nuts, and the ultimate sweetness of whipped cream. It delights all the senses. What more could you ask for in a dessert?"

He chuckled and slowly closed the distance between them. He stood before her, gazing down at her and thinking how lovely she looked in the morning, her face the color of fresh cream. "I've never gotten aroused simply by listening to the ingredients of a hot fudge sundae," he mused aloud. He reached for a strand of hair and rubbed it between his fingers. "What d'you say we grab a can of whipped cream and go upstairs?"

Michelle laughed, but came willingly into his arms. When he looked at her, her stomach felt as though it were coated with hot fudge. He nuzzled her ear, and she shivered and slipped her arms around his waist. He pulled away, his smile gone. His expression was almost tender.

"Mic, I can't do all those things. You know, the grocery store and dry cleaner."

She nodded. "I know that."

"That doesn't mean I'm not wild about you, though. Hell, I think I've been in love with you for fifteen years, but I could never be all those things to you. I reckon I'll always be a selfish bastard, huh?"

She stroked his cheek. "But you're an honest one."

He shook his head. "Lord, I want to make love to you so bad I hurt. I can't look at you without wanting to touch you. And I can't touch you without wanting to taste you. It's like an addiction, Mic." He smiled ruefully. "I don't have any right to make love to you, though. I have nothing to offer, nothing that really matters to a woman like you."

He paused and gazed down at her. Then, because he couldn't help himself, he lowered his lips to hers. He kissed her deeply, his tongue delving into her mouth hungrily. He wanted her. He wanted to sink into her softness and bury his face between her breasts. And it didn't matter that he'd only recently crawled out of her bed. When he raised his head, his eyes glittered from the heat of his need. "Of course I've never let right and wrong stand in the way of taking what I wanted. I suppose there's a good side to being selfish."

Michelle snaked her arms around his shoulders and locked her hands behind his neck. "I suppose," she said softly knowing that she wanted him to make love to her again just as badly as he did. She couldn't get enough of him.

It wasn't purely sexual between them, she knew, but Gator Landry would never admit it. He opened up in bed, something he had difficulty doing otherwise. In bed, he revealed himself for what he truly was—kind and loving and very giving. But she knew he was hell-bent on preserving his tough-as-nails image. Gator had a gentle side that tugged at her heartstrings and wouldn't let go. And although he might balk at the idea of spending too much time with one woman, she knew he was hers in bed. For one heart-stopping moment, as he shuddered against her, he was totally and completely hers. And she didn't need false promises from him. For the moment, the man himself was more than enough.

Gator lifted her easily into his arms and carried her up the stairs to the bedroom. He lowered her onto the bed gently, then began undressing her, kissing each spot he bared.

When she was completely naked, she raised up and began taking off his clothes. There was something very sensual about undressing him, she thought, peeling his snug jeans from his thighs. She swallowed a lump in her throat when she caught sight of the evidence of his desire.

Michelle knelt on the floor between his thighs and kissed him then, taking his tongue into her mouth lovingly. She caressed his calves, as she deepened the kiss. And then he groaned and pulled away, and a moment later they were both on the bed, instantly swept up in a tide of white-hot passion that left them clinging to each other afterward, chanting each other's names on breathless sighs.

Gator held her for a long time, listening to the sound of his own heartbeat, interrupted here and there by birdcalls from outside the window. When he spoke, his voice was low. "I want you to know this has been the best two days of my life," he confessed. He squeezed her. "Thank you, Mic." He pondered his own words. He'd never thanked a woman for sharing his bed before. He'd bought them gifts, yes. But he owed her something more than just a slap on the back after what they'd shared. She'd given him more than a good time. He sensed she'd given of herself as well. Compared to that, a simple thank you didn't seem enough.

Michelle was genuinely touched by his words,

but she didn't answer right away. She didn't trust her voice at the moment. Her throat kept filling up with lumps and her heart ached, knowing that in a matter of time she would have to leave Gator's bed, the one place he could feel secure loving her. And she felt he truly loved her, had loved her for years, just as she had loved him. Yes, loved him, she told herself. She was in love with Gator Landry; it was as simple as that.

She raised herself up on one elbow and smiled into the handsome face. "I should be thanking you. It's not often a girl gets to splurge on hot fudge sundaes, you know." And it wasn't often a man made a woman feel the way he had made her feel. Gator had touched her in ways other men hadn't come close to, both physically and emotionally. He had branded her as his as surely as if he'd stuck a hot iron to her hide and singed his initials there. Nothing and nobody would ever come close to him in her heart. But that shouldn't surprise her, she told herself. He'd been doing it to her since she was fifteen. Although he had not slept with her back then, he'd been the man who had awakened her body, brought sweet yearnings to the surface. With softly spoken words and gentle touches, he had sent sensual messages to her brain that had never died. Instead, they'd slipped back into her subconscious, where they'd laid waiting all these years to be kindled to life.

She had screwed up royally this time, she told herself. She had gone and fallen in love with Gator Landry. But hadn't she suspected it would happen sooner or later if she spent much time with him? Wasn't that the real reason she hadn't returned the following summer as she'd promised all those years ago, the reason she'd avoided him completely on subsequent visits to her grandmother's? She had known at fifteen how volatile the attraction between them was, how dangerous, but mostly she had realized that nothing could become of their relationship. Even at fifteen, Gator's need for independence had been firmly embedded in his personality. He might chase her relentlessly, but he would always remain just beyond her grasp. She would spend her life regretting her love for the man, she decided. It was probably a lot like loving a married man, she supposed. He was only able to offer so much and nothing more. Gator had made it plain what he could and could not offer her.

A grinding noise broke through the silence in the room, and Michelle jumped. Gator rose from the bed and walked to the window, unabashed in his nakedness. "A boat," he said. "Somebody finally decided to come for us."

Michelle was thankful, almost.

"Well, they don't look any different," Reba said to Fiona as Gator and Michelle climbed out of his pickup truck and headed for the house.

Fiona Landry blushed. "Shhh, they'll hear you!"

Reba planted her spindly hands on her hips and regarded the two with an amused look. "It's a crying shame when you got to send the rescue squad out to pick up folks just 'cause they ain't got enough sense to come home when they're 'posed to."

Gator hugged his mother. "Hope I didn't worry you, Mom," he said. "There was a problem with the boat."

Fiona waved the remark aside. "Oh, I wasn't worried. I reckon there's not a soul alive who knows the bayou better than you. Now, come up here on the porch and have something cold to drink. You too, Michelle. I hope my son has been behaving himself."

Michelle blushed in spite of herself. If only the woman knew. A brief picture of Gator and herself tangled in the bed sheets flashed through her mind. "Yes, he was a perfect gentleman, Mrs. Landry." She didn't see the look of disappoint-ment on the older ladies' faces, nor the amuse-ment lurking in Gator's eyes.

"What's this 'Mrs. Landry' nonsense?" the woman asked. "You call me Fiona, y'hear?" She led Michelle onto the front porch and seated her. "How about a cold glass of iced tea?" she asked. "And some of my sugar cookies." "I made these cookies the morning of the storm, just in case we lost power and I couldn't bake for a spell," she added, holding out a plate. "Here, son, you sit yourself down next to Michelle and tell me and Reba all about your adventures the last couple of days."

"Well, there's not much to tell," Gator said, tak-ing the rocker next to Michelle's and feeling as though he'd just been summoned to the princi-pal's. He didn't notice the fallen expressions on the women's faces. "I killed a snake. I reckon that's the most exciting thing that happened." He turned to Michelle for confirmation. "Wouldn't you say?"

She blushed again and almost choked on her cookie. "Uh, yes." She offered a faint smile. "A cottonmouth," she added to cover her embarrassment. Lord, she had never felt so guilty in her life. She and Gator must look as though they come straight from a Roman orgy, Michelle thought to herself. And to think how the poor women had worried about them. Probably hadn't slept all night. "It looked to be four or five feet long," she said.

Fiona patted Michelle's hand. "I'll bet you were scared to death, honey," she said. "But it's over now, and Reba and I have been toting water into the bathroom for two solid hours so you could have that bubble bath I promised you yesterday. Nothing like a nice hot bubble bath to lift your spirits."

"Gator prepared a bubble bath for me last night," Michelle said without thinking. The two elderly ladies exchanged hopeful looks. "He even helped me wash my hair over the bathroom sink." The women almost grinned from ear to ear at that remark.

Gator cleared his throat and stood, as though uncomfortable with the silence that followed Michelle's declaration. "I reckon I better get into town and see what's going on," he said.

"You're coming back for dinner, aren't you?" Fiona asked. "Reba and I killed two fat hens—"

"I don't think so, Mom. I really need to help in town." Gator knew he was merely making excuses, but he'd spent too much time with Michelle already. He couldn't even look at her without getting butterflies in his stomach, a sensation that was totally new to him, and he was too old to walk around with a sick, dreamy-eyed expression on his face. Besides, she would be going home in a day or two, and he refused to make a fool of himself in the meantime.

"But son, you have to come," Fiona said. "You know I don't know the first thing about cooking chicken on a barbecue grill."

"That's right," Reba said, joining in. "And after what your mama and I went through to catch and prepare those chickens, the least you can do is cook them for us."

Gator felt himself weakening. "I guess I can come back for a little while," he said hesitantly, at the same time wondering if his mother realized she was putting him in an awkward position. He could feel Michelle's eyes on him. Hell, she probably figured he owed it to her to hang around while she was in town. He'd never met a woman yet who didn't get possessive once things turned intimate. "But I can't stay long," he added quickly. Maybe he'd drop by the Night Life Lounge and see if his buddy needed any help getting the place on its feet again. He glanced at Michelle. Yeah, she was watching him, her neck tilted to the side, studying him the way a chicken would a fat worm. "See you," he said, and bounded down the porch toward his truck. He disappeared down the road in a cloud of red dust.

Michelle watched him go, feeling a dullness in the pit of her stomach at the sight of his retreating vehicle. For some reason he seemed in a big hurry to leave, and it irritated her. But it didn't surprise her. She was just disappointed that he hadn't been more subtle in his need to escape. He hadn't spoken a handful of words to her since they'd left Reba's house. Heck, he couldn't even look her in the eye. All her insecurities threatened to surface, and she knew if she let them, she'd be a basket case before it was over. There wasn't anything wrong with her, she decided. Gator Landry was simply running scared.

"Now, dear, how about the bath?" Fiona asked, putting her arms around Michelle's shoulders. "You know, I feel as if I've known you all my life. Reba has told me so much about you."

Chatting easily with the woman, Michelle followed her inside the house and to the bathroom, where a tub waited, filled with scented water. Her mind instantly replayed images of the tub Gator had prepared for her the night before with dish detergent, of Gator sitting next to her on the couch wearing only a bathrobe that showed off his powerful thighs and calves, of Gator leaning over her, his hair-roughened body brushing against her.

"You shouldn't have gone to so much trouble," Michelle told the woman, trying to block the sensual pictures.

"Gator fixed me a place out back to cook on till the power comes back," Fiona said. "He's quite handy, you know."

"Yes, I know," Michelle said dully. At the look

on Fiona's face, she added hurriedly. "He did the same at Reba's. I think the man works too hard, if you ask me."

Fiona nodded. "Well, we have to do what we can to get by, dear." She reached into a cabinet and pulled out a fluffy towel and washcloth, and Michelle could tell they were new or almost new. The woman probably saved them for company.

"Thank you, Mrs. Landry. I mean, Fiona."

Fiona smiled. "Now you enjoy your bath. There are magazines under the sink you can read if you like. Oh, and I'll look around and see if I can find something for you to wear. You and I wear close to the same size, I think. I'll just drape it over the doorknob when I find something."

Michelle emerged from the bathroom more than an hour later wearing one of Fiona's dresses, a simple cotton shift that made her feel as cool as she looked. The fit wasn't bad, she noted, but the sandals were too wide for her feet. Michelle kicked them off and decided to go barefoot instead. She pulled her hair up into the French braid she often wore to work, and when she entered the kitchen, Fiona and Reba applauded her efforts.

"Now if I only had my makeup," Michelle said laughingly. "I feel naked without it."

"Did I hear you mention makeup?" Fiona asked, raising two brows. She stood and motioned for Michelle to follow her into her bedroom. She opened a drawer and presented Michelle with an old cigar box.

"I don't wear makeup often so I don't know if it's still good. But you're welcome to it."

Michelle glanced inside the box and found several items she could use. "Thank you," she said. "I'll put the box back when I'm finished."

This time when Michelle came out, there was a glow to her face. She'd used the makeup sparingly but had applied just enough to bring out her green eyes and put a rosy blush on her cheeks.

Fiona smiled. "There, dear. Feel better?"

"Much better, thanks." Michelle rubbed her hands together. "Now, what can I do to help?"

"You can sit here at this table and tell me all the damage that's been done to my house, for one thing," Reba said. "How about another glass of iced tea? We have to use this ice before it melts. Won't get no more 'fore tomorrow, you know."

While Michelle sipped the tea, she told the women of the progress she and Gator had made on the house. "Gator has promised to see to the cats, Grand," Michelle added, "but I don't think you should rush back anytime soon. At least wait until your power is restored."

"Reba and I have discussed it, and she's agreed to stay with me," Fiona said. "She has no business out there in the boonies with no electricity or telephone."

"I've been pleading with her for years to have a phone installed," Michelle said. "Maybe this time she'll agree to do it."

"I said I would, didn't I?" Reba replied, obviously weary of the subject. "Besides, I reckon I done spent enough time alone. Fiona showed me how much I miss having folks to talk to. I just didn't want much to do with people after your grandfather died."

They talked for a while, then Fiona took

Michelle on a tour of the house. Everything was as cheery as the kitchen, decorated in splashes of yellow and white. Crisp white curtains billowed at the windows and thriving plants adorned every available table and shelf. Fiona opened the door to Gator's old bedroom, and Michelle stepped inside.

What surprised her most was the number of books in the room. One wall had been devoted entirely to book cases, upon which rested a variety of paperbacks, ranging from mystery and detective stories to horror novels. Interspersed among them was an odd asortment—books on reptiles and fish, time management, extrasensory perception.

"Matthieu loved to read as a child," Fiona said. "He wasn't crazy about his schoolbooks, but the boy must've read every mystery ever written. He was a bit of a loner, I reckon. Never had any real close friends."

Michelle nodded, taking in the old record player and albums that lined another shelf. She thumbed through his record collection, finding country-western, hard rock, and a couple of gospel albums. She felt like a snoop, but she was hoping his personal things would offer some insight into the man. They didn't. The real Gator Landry was neatly tucked inside the man, and she doubted if he'd ever let anyone really see him. She glanced up at the twin bed with its old-fashioned quilt that she knew Fiona had made. Over the bed hung a simple wooden crucifix, its polished surface glinting in the afternoon sun.

"Matthieu was such a neat boy," Fiona said, absently straightening a picture on the wall. "His father was very particular. Everything had to be in its place." She chuckled. "I'm afraid I've grown a bit lax since his death."

"The place looks great to me," Michelle said.

"I'd rather be working in my garden or the flower beds," the woman confessed. She smiled suddenly. "Come outside and see my flowers. Or should I say what's left of them since the storm."

For the next hour or so, while Reba relaxed on the front porch, Michelle followed Fiona over the grounds as the woman pointed out various flowers and shrubs she'd planted and nurtured over the years. Michelle was amused listening to Fiona rattle off the history of each plant as if it were a member of the family. They ended up spending the better part of the afternoon working in the flower beds, spraying and pruning Fiona's rosebushes, tying back those that had been damaged in the storm.

"You're pretty good at this," Fiona said once they'd done all they could for the roses.

Michelle smiled. "I used to help Grand with her gardening when I was a child. I've always loved flowers. I must have two dozen house plants at home."

Fiona nodded. "You in a hurry to get back?"

"My job is very important to me."

"Everyone needs something meaningful in their life," Fiona said. "I don't know what I'd do without my flowers and my church work." She paused. "But I think a family is important too, don't you?"

Michelle thought it odd that the woman had brought up the subject, but she merely shrugged.

"With the right man, I suppose. But I haven't met anyone I'd care to spend the rest of my life with."

"Maybe you aren't looking hard enough."

Michelle laughed at the serious expression on Fiona's face. "I'm not advertising in the personals column, if that's what you mean. But most men don't seem to have a sincere interest in marriage and family these days."

Fiona smiled and plucked a perfect rosebud that had a miraculously survived the storm. She handed it to Michelle. "Men are a lot like roses, dear. They each have their share of thorns that make it tough to get close to them. And their hearts are just as delicate and fragile as a rose petal, believe it or not. But with the right amount of love and nurturing and understanding, they too can blossom into something wonderful."

Michelle gazed at the rose thoughtfully. "What a lovely comparison, Fiona. You should write poetry."

The woman laughed and waved the statement aside. "You look tired, dear," she said to Michelle after awhile. "Why don't you rest now."

It sounded like a great idea to Michelle. "I think I'll lie on that chaise lounge in the shade," she said. "Unless there's something else I can do to help you."

"Go ahead," Fiona said, shooing her in that direction. "You've done enough work."

Michelle didn't need further prompting. Still clutching the rose between her fingers, she crossed the backyard to the lounge chair that sat beneath a giant oak. She adjusted the back into a reclining position and lay down, crossing her long legs at the ankles.

So peaceful, she thought, hearing the screen door close behind Fiona as the woman went back into the house. A breeze rustled the leaves overhead and fanned her cheek. She closed her eyes. She wasn't surprised when Gator's face came into view, and she wondered if she would ever be able to close her eyes without seeing that rugged face.

An hour later Gator made his way across the backyard toward the garage, where he knew his mother kept the barbecue grill. He came to a screeching halt when he spotted Michelle sleeping in the chair. He stepped closer.

She looked clean and fresh in a blue and white summer dress, and her face was as delicate in sleep as the rose in her lap. Her hair had been pulled back, but some of it had escaped, and blond tendrils wafted over her face in the breeze. She had never looked lovelier. He slid his gaze downward to her slender legs and smiled at the sight of her bare feet. Her eyelashes fluttered open then, and she appeared surprised at finding him there.

"Did I fall asleep?"

He nodded. "Looks that way."

"Oh." She raised up and patted her hair self-consciously. "I must've been more tired than I thought."

Her words seemed to amuse him. "You didn't get much sleep last night, as I recall."

She blushed. No man had ever made her blush

so much in her life. She wondered how long he'd been watching her. "When did you get here?"

"Just this minute. My mother sent me out to find the grill, with firm instructions not to wake you."

Michelle noticed he'd changed clothes. He looked good in a short-sleeve cotton print shirt and the usual blue jeans. "Is there anything I can do to help?"

He didn't answer right away. "You could do one thing, Mic," he said at last. "You could stop tempting me beyond rational thought. You could stop haunting my dreams at night. That would help a great deal." With that he walked away.

Nine

Michelle couldn't remember when chicken had tasted so good. By the time Gator had forked the sizzling meat from the grill, her mouth had been watering. After having spent the past few days eating hot dogs and canned tuna and Spam, the grilled chicken was a real treat. Fiona had picked some of the last of her vegetables from the garden and, of course, there was also the old standby these days, pork and beans from a can. Michelle took a serving out of politeness but decided she'd eaten enough pork and beans to last a lifetime. Gator had brought a bag of ice from town, so they sipped iced tea with their meal and felt privileged to have it.

Gator was surprisingly quiet over dinner, although he gave a progress report on the work in town. A group of Mennonites had arrived that afternoon with several truckloads of lumber and planned to work as long as necessary to get people back into their homes. Donations had already started pouring in, through both the Red Cross and from private citizens trying to assist the homeless. An anonymous caller had donated a brand-new mobile home for a family of six who'd lost their trailer when part of the mobile-home park had been destroyed, and although it would take a couple of weeks for the trailer to arrive, Gator and the town's officials hoped it would spark more donations.

It was dark by the time they finished dinner, and while Michelle assisted the women in cleaning up, Gator lit the kerosene lamps. Michelle sensed the change in him. He was withdrawing, she knew. It was clear by the way he avoided eye contact with her, by the way he was careful not to stand too close, by the way he walked clear around the table to avoid brushing past her. And it irritated the daylights out of her. All her insecurities threatened to surface, but she forced them back. She was not going to let Gator's behavior upset her, she told herself. She did not deserve it. She had given him the best part of her. She had known him more intimately than any man before, and if he chose to back off, that was his problem.

It had been good between them—downright wonderful, as a matter of fact. Perhaps that was the problem. Maybe Gator realized he wasn't likely to find it so good anywhere else. Something had clicked between them, not only physically, but emotionally. And Gator knew that, she was certain. She had seen it in his eyes, felt it in his tender kiss, heard it in his sighs of pleasure.

Gator could deny it all he wanted, but deep down he had to recognize it for what it was—love. Still, she would bite her tongue off before she'd try to convince him. She would never push or try to extract promises from him. Heaven knew, she'd had enough of that from her parents, always vying for their attention, living on false promises, playing second fiddle to their busy careers and social life.

It hadn't been much better with Jeffrey. With him, medicine and his patients had come first. All his energies had been geared to that cause, and by the time he could schedule an evening with her, he was emotionally drained. She had not minded at first, so impressed was she with his dedication to others. But now she realized he'd spent a great deal of time whining to her about it afterward or breaking dates simply because he was too exhausted to do anything. And she had been exhausted too, having worked right alongside him. Yet, somehow that fact had escaped him. She had been shortchanged in the relationship, she knew. Just as she'd been shortchanged in her dealings with her parents. She didn't feel sorry for herself any longer, thank heavens, but she was determined not to let it happen again. From now on, she would get back what she gave to a man. She would come first in his life or not at all.

"Why don't we sit on the front porch for a bit?" Fiona suggested, interrupting Michelle's thought. The older woman untied her cotton apron and folded it. "It's much cooler out there."

Gator had a refusal formed on his lips but bit

it back. He couldn't very well rush off without appearing rude. He would stay ten or fifteen minutes, then excuse himself, saying he had to get back to town. He knew it was crazy to stay. He hadn't been able to keep his eyes off Michelle all evening, and every time she caught him staring he glanced away. He felt like a teenager again, trying to catch her scent as she passed by him. He would have half the town laughing at him behind his back by the time she returned home.

Reba and Fiona carried the conversation for a while; then, as though perfectly synchronized, they stood and excused themselves, announcing they were ready for bed. The screen door slammed closed behind them, and Gator suddenly found himself alone with Michelle.

He gazed at her for a moment, tracing her silhouette in the moonlight. Her neck looked long and sleek with her hair pulled back. He was tempted to loosen her hair from the knot so he could watch it fall to her shoulders. His gut tightened at the thought of how she'd looked in bed with her hair fanning the pillow.

He should tell her how he was feeling, he thought. Tell her why he had to put some distance between them. It wasn't fair just leaving her hanging as he'd done with other women so many times before. This wasn't just any woman—this was Michelle, the girl he'd dreamed about for fifteen years. He owed her the truth. But before he could say anything, she stood and stretched.

"I think I'll turn in now," she said, giving him an easy smile. "I need to be up early in the morning and get into town. I want to see what can be done about my car." She patted Gator on the shoulder as she passed, much as she would have a brother or an old school buddy. She didn't see his look of surprise. "Good night, Gator." And then she was gone.

For a moment, Gator merely sat there, staring at the chair she'd occupied only a moment before. He had planned his exit so carefully, rehearsed exactly what he'd say if she tried to pressure him or stop him from leaving. Oddly enough, she hadn't asked him about the future, nor had she made any reference to the time they'd spent alone at Reba's place. He hadn't had to lie or make excuses or any of the usual stuff.

And he didn't quite know what to make of it.

Gator pushed himself up from the rocker and headed toward his truck, a frown drawing his brows together. He drove toward town, passing the Night Life Lounge, where a dozen or so cars were parked out front. Knowing the owner as he did, Gator figured the man would have iced down a couple of cases and was serving by candlelight. He braked, thinking he might stop by for a cold one and a bit of conversation.

He pulled off the road and sat in the parking lot for a full five minutes, trying to decide what to do. Well, why not go inside and pop a can, he thought. He was off duty and had put in a rough day. He deserved to kick up his feet and relax a bit. Of course, he would be expected to flirt and carry on with the women as he usually did—he hadn't let a sheriff's badge change him in that department.

But he *had* changed in other ways, he knew.

He had fallen in love with Michelle Thurston all over again, and he was half-afraid someone would discover it, either in his face or in the way he talked. And how would he carry on an intelligent conversation, for Pete's sake? He couldn't think straight these days, and he hadn't had a decent night's sleep since Michelle had hit town. Boy, falling in love really took it out of a guy, he decided.

Once again, he told himself he had to get her out of town. Until then, he would have to put his partying aside. He didn't need a beer when he was confused to begin with. And he didn't need loud music or conversation when his thoughts were so jumbled he couldn't see his hands in front of his face.

Gator accelerated, pulling out of the parking lot and leaving the lounge behind, and he silently cursed the green-eyed woman who'd reduced him to such a sad state.

When Gator carried a bag of ice out to his mother's the following afternoon, he learned that Michelle had gotten up early and driven Fiona's car into town. She returned just as he was about to leave, her expression almost forlorn.

"Did you find someone to help you with your car?" he asked as she climbed out of his mother's old station wagon.

"They can't get to it until next week," she said. "It's going to take them a few more days to repair the bridge. Needless to say, they can't get to my car until the bridge is safe to cross. Then I have to wait my turn. My car was not the only one damaged in the storm," she added with a dejected sigh.

Gator crossed his arms and leaned against his truck. He couldn't help feeling a little sorry for her. She was wearing the same blue and white striped dress from the day before, her hair pulled into a demure ponytail, making her appear years younger. He realized then just how disappointed he'd been when he'd arrived and found her gone.

He hadn't slept worth a damn the night before, tossing and turning in his bed until the wee hours of the morning, his thoughts, as always, trained on Michelle. He wondered if she guessed what he was going through, the emptiness that stole over him when she wasn't around, the fear and frustration of seeing her and knowing nothing could come of their relationship. He wondered if she was going through any of it herself, but decided she probably wasn't. She was in such an all-fired hurry to get back home she probably had no idea how much he was suffering.

On one hand, he wanted her so badly he couldn't stand it. He wanted to feel her beneath him, opening herself up to him—just as his mother's roses opened their petals to receive the sun. He wanted to fill her with his own heat. He wanted to slip his tongue between those dewy lips of hers, hear her sigh of pleasure at his ear, feel her body tremble at his touch, and listen to the tiny gasping sound she made each time she climaxed. He wanted to reach out in his sleep and find her there, soft and warm and smelling like a piece of heaven. Once again, he chided himself for having such dangerous thoughts.

It irritated the hell out of him that he could wallow in indecision and utter bewilderment while she couldn't wait to get back to her life in Baton Rouge, to the doctor in his spiffy white lab coat and prestigious lifestyle. And why should he care? She'd made it plain she preferred the consistency of an apple-pie relationship to what he had to offer—a fickle, unreliable diet of ice cream sundaes.

He had decided the night before to hand in his resignation at the end of the week. That in itself would take a big load off his mind, and by then the townspeople would at least be headed in the right direction. Although it would still be a couple of weeks before power was restored, at least the people of Lizard Thicket would have the necessities. What more could they expect from him? he'd asked himself. Not a damn thing more, he'd decided.

But there was still the problem of what to do about Michelle. She was a constant distraction to him. With her out of the way, his life could get back to normal again. He could gear his thoughts in the right direction once more. He hadn't spent ten years of his life sweating his butt off in the sugar cane fields only to end up just like his father, chasing poachers through the swamps, busting up barroom brawls, risking his neck every time a husband and wife got into a heated argument. For the first time in his life he had money to travel with, money to invest in something lucrative. He could go places and do things he'd never dreamed of before. He could *be* somebody, despite having lived with a man much of his life who had claimed he'd never amount to anything. But first, he had to put Michelle out of his life—this time for good.

"I'll take you home, Mic," he finally said, surprising himself as much as her with his words. But he'd already promised to help her. It was the least he could do.

"You?"

He nodded. "It might take a couple of weeks for someone to get to your car." He knew she'd never be able to wait. "Could you manage without it for a while?"

She shrugged. "I suppose I could catch a ride to work with one of the other nurses."

"I'm sure you'll find someone to give you a lift," he said, wondering whether her doctor friend would be the one to accommodate her. "You'll have to come back for your car later."

Michelle pondered his offer. The man was obviously in a hurry to get rid of her, if he was willing to drive her all the way back to Baton Rouge personally. "When can you take me?" she asked.

Gator shoved his hands in his pockets. She'd jumped at the offer, just as he'd known she would. "I've got some things to take care of in town this afternoon, but I can drive you back tonight if you like. You'll need to make arrangements about your car before you leave."

Michelle stiffened. The guy wasn't wasting any time getting her out of town. It hurt knowing how anxious he was to see her go, especially after what they'd shared, but she'd be damned if she'd let him know. She smiled brightly. "Thanks, Gator. I'll be ready."

Gator picked Michelle up shortly before six o'clock that evening. She was waiting for him on the front porch, dressed in what looked to be new blue jeans and a crisp white cotton blouse that made her look as fresh as morning sunshine. The jeans hugged her hips nicely and emphasized her trim waist and long legs. He felt his gut tighten when she leaned over to kiss Reba and his mother good-bye, after promising to return for her car in a week or so. Gator planned to be long gone by that time.

"Ready?" he asked when she turned to him.

Michelle nodded, picking up her purse and tossing kisses to the women on the porch. Gator hugged his mother briefly and followed Michelle to his truck. A moment later, they were on their way down the dirt road.

Reba and Fiona didn't speak at first. Finally, Reba turned to the other woman. "What d'you think, Fi? My granddaughter sure is in a hurry to get back. That cain't be a good sign."

"I don't know what to think," Fiona said, shaking her head sadly. "All I know is, my son is head over heels in love with that girl. He's so much in love, he can't see straight."

"Well, that's good, isn't it?" Reba asked.

"Maybe. But they walked away from each other before, y'know."

Reba waved the statement aside. "They were only fifteen years old at the time. Too young to do anything about it."

Fiona sighed, looking tired and sad. "I have a feeling if they walk away from each other again, it'll be for the last time. And my son is just stubborn and hardheaded enough to do something like that."

Gator glanced at Michelle as he drove, wondering why she was so quiet. She was certainly different from most women he knew, who talked nonstop about things that didn't interest him in the least. "Are those new clothes you're wearing?" he asked.

She smiled. "Yes, your mother called a friend of hers who owns one of the dress shops in town, and the lady opened up so I could come in and buy something." She laughed. "It's nice to finally wear clothes that fit."

He wanted to tell her she'd look good in a flour sack six sizes too big, but he didn't. "I'm glad she was able to help," he said instead.

"Your mother is very nice. I like her a lot."

Gator gripped the steering wheel. Wasn't that just like a woman, he told himself. First, she worked on getting a man's mother to like her, then she went after the man with both barrels.

"I'm really pleased your mother and my grandmother hit it off so well," she said. "I worry about Grand out on the bayou all alone. At least she'll have a friend to check on her now and then. And your mother convinced her once and for all to have that telephone installed. I can't tell you what a relief that was."

Gator frowned. For a moment it sounded as if Michelle's relationship with his mother had absolutely nothing to do with him.

They rode in silence for more than an hour. Michelle nodded off and woke with a start when her head fell to the side.

"Tired?" he asked.

She smiled drowsily. "Riding always makes me sleepy. Except when I drive, of course." She yawned wide.

"You can lay your head on my lap and stretch out on the seat if you like."

"That's okay." She yawned again.

"What's the big deal? You look as if you could use some shut-eye. I won't bite."

She blushed. "I know that. I just don't—" She paused.

"Don't what?"

"Don't want you to get the wrong idea."

So she *was* backing off, he told himself, surprised at the fact. Most women would have used the opportunity to cozy up to him, used their feminine wiles to get what they wanted from him. But Michelle wasn't like most women, he'd learned over the past few days. Or maybe he'd known that fifteen years ago. Even then, she'd stood out among the crowd. Still, he couldn't stand to see her uncomfortable, with her head lopping to the side every time she dozed. He hated the position they were in. They'd gone too far to simply be friends.

"Look, Mic," he said, his dark eyes locking with

hers briefly. "I've seen and tasted every inch of you. I don't think it would be out of line for you to lay your head on my lap."

Michelle blushed a bright fuchsia. He really knew how to put things into perspective and make her toes curl at the same time with his blatant remarks. Arguing with the man was pointless, and the fact that she couldn't stop yawning would only prove how sleepy she was and make him think she was afraid of touching him. How could she appear cool and indifferent to him if she acted afraid of his closeness? "Well, if you're sure," she finally said. "I just don't want to get in the way of your driving and all." She rearranged herself in the seat, and Gator raised his elbow so she could slip her head onto his lap.

That was his first mistake, Gator realized the moment her head came in contact with his thigh. He flinched inwardly when her ear brushed his crotch as she attempted to get comfortable. He gripped the steering wheel until his knuckles turned white.

Michelle tried to find comfort against Gator's hard thigh, but she was very much aware of his belt buckle at the back of her head, his zipper pressing against her hair. Her thoughts ran wild. She closed her eyes and tried to block out the sensual images. Thankfully, the sound of the engine and the slight rocking sensations of the truck made her sleepy.

It was all he could do to keep his eyes on the road ahead and not stare at the woman who slept with her head on his lap. He tried counting the exit signs, read billboards, and played a game of solitary cow poker whenever he spotted cattle grazing along the way. Nothing helped. The truck jostled her head slightly from time to time, creating enough friction to keep him thoroughly aroused. His mind ran amok. He imagined her waking, unbuckling his belt, working the zipper open . . . aw, damn!

Michelle awoke with a start when her head bumped the steering wheel, and the truck veered sharply to the right. She grabbed Gator's knee to keep from sliding off the seat and heard him groan.

"What are you doing?" she asked, raising up from his lap and rubbing the sleep from her eyes.

Gator didn't quite meet the look in her eyes. "We're stopping for dinner. There's a great steak restaurant at this exit," he said. "I promised you a steak dinner, remember?"

"Steak?" She said the word as though it were foreign to her.

"Uh-huh." He drove up the ramp and paused at the stop sign.

"With a baked potato swimming in butter and sour cream and sprinkled with green onions and bacon bits?"

Gator was so happy to have her head off his lap, he grinned. "Yep. You can have anything you want."

"And hot garlic bread?" she added hopefully. "And strawberry pie for dessert?"

Gator pulled onto the main road and drove in the direction of the restaurant. "I thought you preferred hot fudge sundaes," he teased.

She slapped him playfully on the arm. "You

naughty boy. Can't you get your mind out of the bedroom *ever*?"

He didn't respond, but it wasn't because he didn't know the answer to her question. As long as she was beside him his mind was permanently fixed on the bedroom and all the delightful things she did to him. And there wasn't a damn thing he could do about it.

Sharing dinner with Michelle was about as sensual as sharing her bed, Gator decided once their food arrived. He watched her, slightly amused, as she slathered enough sour cream on her potato to feed a family of four. She took great delight in swirling it about, mixing it with the creamy butter, bacon bits, onions, and shredded cheese. Once she'd popped a forkfull into her mouth, she leaned back in her chair and closed her eyes dreamily. She attacked her T-bone with a vengeance.

Gator chuckled. "Do you always eat like there's no tomorrow?"

She smiled. "Only when I'm forced to live on canned food for a while." She ended up eating everything on her plate and some of his, then polished off the meal with her favorite, strawberry pie.

"I'm going to have to carry you out to my truck," Gator said laughingly once he'd paid the bill.

"Oh, Lord, I'm waddling like duck," she exclaimed, following him out the door to the parking lot. "I'll have to eat salads and skip dessert for weeks to make up for cheating on my diet like this."

"You could always eat canned tuna," he said. "That's good for diets."

Michelle stopped dead in the middle of the parking lot and threw her hand over her mouth. "Did you have to mention canned tuna?" came her muffled reply.

They reached her apartment shortly after nine o'clock, the day having faded into night. Gator shut off the engine and stared straight ahead at nothing in particular. This was it, he thought. He'd done everything in his power to get her home, and now he didn't know what to do. He wasn't quite ready to let her go.

"Please come in for coffee," she said. "I can't just let you turn around and drive all the way back without coming in for a moment."

He pondered her offer. He really should get back, he told himself. There was a lot of work still left to do before he handed in his badge in a few days. But he couldn't say good-bye that easily to a woman who meant so much to him, to the woman he'd fallen in love with. Not only that, but he was curious. He wanted to see the inside of her apartment, find out how she lived.

"Maybe for a minute," he said at last. "But then I really do have to get back."

Ten

Gator liked her place, although it was a bit prissy for his tastes, with its yellow floral sofa and striped chair of yellow and salmon. On her coffee table was a vase of flowers that had long since died. It made him smile. She looked like the kind of woman who'd like fresh flowers.

Her kitchen was as warm and cheerful as his mother's, with brightly painted wicker baskets adorning one wall and another devoted to gleaming copper cookware. Michelle dumped the dead flowers and went about making coffee.

"Why don't you have a seat in the living room?" she suggested. "It won't take but a minute for the coffee to drip through."

Gator sank onto the fat sofa and leaned back, then kicked off his boots and propped his feet on the coffee table. He thought better of it after a moment and pulled them back down.

"You can put your feet up," Michelle said,

watching him with a smile from the kitchen doorway.

"Thanks. My legs are kind of cramped from riding." He stretched his long legs on the table once more, careful not to disturb the neat stacks of magazines and brass knickknacks.

"It sure is nice to have electricity and running water again," Michelle said a few minutes later as she carried in two cups of steaming coffee. "I should have asked Grand to come back with me."

Gator chuckled. "She wouldn't have left the bayou. It's in her blood."

"But not in yours, right?" she said, offering him a dainty porcelain cup that looked much too small for his big hands. She wished now she had grabbed one of the old mugs that she normally used. She took a seat in the chair across from him.

"Right." With great amusement, Gator studied the cup she'd handed him. He was almost afraid it would crumble in his hands. He thought of the chipped pieces he'd served coffee to her in at his place and was almost embarrassed. He probably should put more thought into his possessions, he told himself, but then realized how useless they were for a man on the go.

"So, have you decided where you'll go when you leave Lizard Thicket?" she asked.

He shrugged. "Who knows? I think I'll just travel for a while."

"I've always wanted to travel. I'd like to see Europe one day."

"You could always come with me."

She didn't know whether he was serious or not,

and she laughed to hide her uncertainty. "I only have two weeks' vacation, Gator."

Another shrug. "Quit your job."

She was clearly surprised by the remark. "And how do I pay my bills, pray tell?"

"I'll pay them."

Their gazes met and locked, but neither of them said anything for a moment. "I couldn't let you do that," she said. "Besides, I'd never just walk out at the hospital and leave them short-handed. And I've invested a lot of years in that place. I'd lose my seniority if I quit." She paused. "Anyway, I'm not much of a traveler. It's okay for vacations, but I enjoy waking up in the same house every morning. I like the feeling of coming home at the end of a workday. To you that probably sounds dull."

"I guess I've never felt I belonged in a certain place," he said. "I've always been a loner, I reckon, but I prefer it that way. That's why I live on a houseboat; I don't have to put up with snoopy neighbors. Or yard work," he added with a laugh.

"Gator?" Michelle set her cup down.

"Yeah?"

"I hope you find what you're looking for."

He set his cup down, pulled his legs from the table, and stuffed his feet into his boots, taking great pains with the simple task to keep from looking at her. "I hope you do too, Mic," he finally said. He stood and shoved his hands in his pockets, not really knowing what to say or do. "I really have to go," he said at last.

Michelle raised herself from the chair and crossed the room to where he stood. She hesitated a moment before she reached for one of his hands and squeezed it, then raised it slowly to her lips and kissed his open palm. "Thanks for everything, Gator." She knew the list was too long to go into.

The simple gesture surprised him as much as it touched him. He closed his fingers around her hand and pulled her into his arms. "Aw, Mic," he said. Then his lips captured hers.

The kiss was long and deep and hungry, and Gator knew he'd been waiting to do just that all day. He wrapped his arms around her and pulled her close, enjoying the feel of her soft body against his. He caught her scent, tasted the inside of her mouth, and it was more than he could stand. "I want you, Mic," he whispered against her mouth when he broke the kiss. "And as hard as I've tried, I can't stop wanting you."

She nodded. "I know."

Without warning, he lifted her high in his arms and carried her to the short hall and through an open door, which he surmised led to the bedroom. He caught a glimpse of a bed draped in soft pastels and ruffles and satin throw pillows trimmed in lace, but he was more interested in the woman in his arms. They fell onto the bed together, arms and legs entwined, each of them grasping at the other's clothing. As soon as they were naked, Gator stripped the bed of its coverlet in one sweeping gesture, then captured Michelle's face in his hands and kissed her deeply.

Their coupling was rowdy and frenzied. Each time they reached the brink, he paused and suckled at her breasts until both nipples were wet and swollen. They climaxed together, both of them calling out as though searching for each other in a fog. Gator ground his hips against her for one shuddering moment, then fell against her limply.

He kissed her then, tenderly, stroking her bottom lip with his tongue, their warm breath uniting just as their bodies had a moment before. They were replete, having feasted well on their love.

Michelle didn't realize she was crying until she felt a tear slide silently down her cheek, and the moment was so bittersweet, she thought her heart would burst from the intensity.

Without a word, Gator rolled off of her, captured her in his arms, and pulled her close. He stared at the ceiling long and hard, as though the bumpy plasterwork held some universal answers to the questions bouncing around in his head. Now and then, he stroked her hair, caressed her shoulder, and waited for the silent tears to stop falling. He hated himself for what he was doing to her, hated the fact that their lives were so different. He could not envision Michelle by his side, living on a houseboat in some mosquito-infested swamp, any more than he could imagine her living his day-to-day existence, picking up and moving on whenever the urge hit. She belonged in a neat little house with a perfectly manicured lawn and a husband who came home to her every night. She deserved babies and fresh flowers and a place to store her delicate treasures. She deserved a better man than he could ever be.

For a long time they merely lay there, each of them caught up in their own thoughts. Finally,

Michelle drifted off to sleep. She was vaguely aware when Gator climbed quietly from the bed and stepped into his clothes. She feigned sleep when he kissed her tenderly on her forehead, and she didn't budge when she heard the front door close behind him. Her heart felt heavy, like a water-filled balloon, and she knew a very important chapter in her life had been closed forever. She sighed and reached for the alarm clock on her nightstand. Tomorrow she would go back to work, and somehow, somehow, she'd get through this.

She and Gator had lived the dream that had begun so long ago. Now it was time to go on with their lives.

Gator's mood was dark when he arrived at his office the following morning, after having slept only a couple of hours the night before. He had arrived home sometime after midnight, drank a couple of cold beers, and gone to bed with hopes of catching up on his sleep. It had proved fruitless. Every time he closed his eyes he saw Michelle's tearstained face. He really was a selfish son of a bitch, he told himself.

His office was a hole in the wall, with two jail cells and a couple of battered metal desks. He stepped inside and was surprised to find several teenagers sitting on the hard plastic chairs in the waiting area, none of them more than thirteen or fourteen years old. His deputy came to attention at the sight of him.

"You got visitors, sheriff," he said.

"So I see." Gator regarded the group of boys with an obvious lack of interest. They were refugees from the pool hall he'd closed down. "What can I do for you?" he asked, going over to his desk and sitting down. He propped his legs up and waited as all three approached him.

"You're Sheriff Landry, ain't you?" one of them said.

"That's right."

"My name's Billy Wilcox. This here is Ted and Bart Johnston."

"I know who you are," Gator said curtly. "What do you want?"

"You closed down the pool hall."

"Yeah, I did."

Billy folded his arms over his chest. "Mind telling us why?"

"Because it was nothing but a roach-infested dump, that's why. And because I found drugs and alcohol in the place. I don't like troublemakers, and I don't like punks who get all liquored up and harass the elderly." He narrowed his gaze. "And I especially don't like you roughing up my own mother. Any more questions?"

"Yeah. Mind telling us where we're supposed to go now without a pool hall?"

He shrugged, but he would have given his last dime to know which of them had gone after his mother.

Billy Wilcox's face reddened. "Look, we didn't touch your old lady. The guy responsible for messin' with the old people is long gone now, moved up north. It ain't fair to punish the rest of us because of what he did."

Gator didn't know whether to believe him or not, and he was almost sorry to hear that his mother's attacker might have left town before he could get his hands on him. But it would explain why there hadn't been any recent robberies of the town's older citizens. "Okay, so what d'you want me to do?"

"We want the pool hall reopened."

"No."

"We'll clean it up, get rid of the roaches."

Gator was clearly surprised. He studied the boy for a moment, thinking he was kind of gutsy for coming in to talk to him. He could almost see himself in those defiant eyes, the stubborn tilt of the chin. "Then what? Go back to selling drugs?"

The boy pondered Gator's question. "You could always get someone to look after the place and see that nobody brings anything illegal in."

Gator scoffed at the idea. "What am I supposed to do, come over and baby-sit every day? I don't have that kind of time. Besides—" He paused. "I'm going to be leaving town the end of the week. You'll have to wait and talk to the new person in charge."

The boy twisted his lips in a derisive smile. "Yeah, folks said you'd never stay. Who you gonna get to take your place, some jerk like we had before who was more interested in lining his palms with money than seeing to the problems around here?" He didn't give Gator a chance to answer. "Nobody really gives a damn about what happens to this town," he said. "I think you just took the job so you could get back at the person who robbed your mother. You closed down the pool hall without a thought as to what we were supposed to do for entertainment in this hick town. You're no better than the sheriff we had before you, and you'll never be as good as your father." The boy had to pause to catch his breath. he glanced at his friends. "C'mon, let's get out of here. He can't help us." A moment later they slammed out the door.

Gator's deputy shook his head. "Smart-aleck kid. Somebody needs to take a hickory stick to his hide and teach him some manners."

"I don't know," Gator said, staring at the door through which the boys had just exited. He felt as though he'd been kicked in the gut. "Maybe the kid knows what he's talking about."

Michelle eyed Jeffrey over the rim of her coffee cup as she sat across from him in the hospital cafeteria that afternoon. He hadn't stopped whining and complaining since they'd taken their seats. Her head ached. They'd had bus-accident victims in early that morning, and they had just finished with the last patient. She'd been too tired to eat, so she'd taken only a cup of coffee from the line, hoping the caffeine would revive her.

". . . I just can't take it anymore, Michelle," Jeffrey said, covering his eyes with one hand. "I don't know what I saw in the woman in the first place. All she does is cry and complain. Her ankles are swollen, she can't sleep at night, and she has indigestion all the time. It's driving me up the wall."

"Pregnant women are very emotional, Jeffrey," she said. "You'll just have to be patient."

"You wouldn't act like that, Michelle. You're always so cool and calm. You'd just accept it and try to make the best of it."

She offered him a wry smile. "Don't be too sure about that. I'm sure I'll do my share of complaining when the time comes."

Jeffrey didn't seem to be listening. "I thought I'd go crazy while you were gone," he went on. "If you leave me like that again, I'll never forgive you."

"You shouldn't be saying these things to me, Jeffrey. You should be saying them to your wife."

"Yeah, right." His tone was sarcastic.

"You made the decision to marry her."

"I had no choice."

"Everybody has choices." She was surprised by her own words. Now where had she heard that before? She smiled softly when he looked at her with a hurt expression. "I'm not always going to be around, you know. In fact—" She paused again. "I spoke with the director of nursing when I came in this morning, and she informed me there were some openings in O.R."

"What would you have to do?"

"I'll have to train for six months to qualify for the job. I think the change would be good for me."

"Why didn't you tell me?"

"I didn't have a chance once the bus-accident victims arrived."

"You mean you just agreed to it without talking with me?"

"I didn't see any reason to discuss it with you first."

He leaned forward. "But, Michelle, I need you in emergency. You're the best nurse I've got. How can you do this to me?" He sounded desperate.

Michelle was clearly surprised by his response. The man acted as though her decision were a personal attack against him, when, in fact, it had absolutely nothing to do with him. He obviously hadn't listened all those times she'd told him she needed a change, all those times she'd shared her goals with him. But then, he'd always been so wrapped up in his own problems, how could he have possibly heard hers?

"I'm sorry, Jeffrey, but I can't put my life on hold simply because you need a shoulder to cry on from time to time." She hoped she wasn't being cruel, but she had to finally say what she'd been thinking for months, get it off her chest. Jeffrey, obviously stunned, merely sat there and stared at her. She pushed her chair from the table and stood. "Now, if you'll excuse me, I think I'll get a sandwich before I go back. Would you care for anything?"

He looked like a child who'd just had his favorite toy taken away. "No thanks. I've suddenly lost my appetite."

She smiled and patted him on the shoulder. "It'll come back. And tomorrow you'll have a whole new set of problems to fret about." She hurried to the serving line, leaving him slumped in his chair.

*   *   *

Gator slammed the telephone down so hard, both deputies glanced up from their paperwork in surprise. One of them grinned.

"What's s'matter, still cain't get her?"

Gator shot him a dark look. "I don't know what you're talking about."

The deputy chuckled and ran one meaty hand over his balding head. "You ain't foolin' nobody, Sheriff. We all know you're chasin' after some woman from Baton Rouge. What's the problem?"

Gator crossed his arms over his chest. He was making a fool out of himself over Michelle, just as he'd known he would. How could she have done this to him, reduced him to a sniveling, lovesick adolescent? She'd been gone one week now, and he was going crazy. He was certain the whole town was having a good laugh over it, especially the folks at the Night Life Lounge, since he never stopped by anymore. Twice now he'd driven six blocks out of his way just to keep from passing it. If his friends found out he was going home every night to pine away over some woman, he'd never live it down.

"She's never home," Gator finally said. "That's the problem."

"Oh, so she's got a busy social life, eh?"

Gator shrugged. "I figure she's working. You know how nurses are, dedicated and all."

The deputy snickered, but swallowed his laughter when Gator glowered at him. "Yeah, you're probably right, Sheriff," he agreed.

"And she's involved in some youth program up there. It takes a lot of her time." Gator didn't know who he was trying to convince, his deputy or himself.

Gator shoved his chair from his desk and stood. He had no idea why he was trying to call Michelle in the first place. What would he say? He had rehearsed it in his mind a dozen times, but he hadn't gotten past the part of just wanting to hear her voice.

He needed something to take his mind off her, he thought, until he made some decisions. Decisions that he should have made a week ago. Getting her out of town hadn't helped. All he did these days when he got off work was sit on the deck of his houseboat and stare off into space. His mother had asked him twice if he was coming down with something. Every time he closed his eyes he saw Michelle as she'd looked that morning he'd left her lying in her bed, pretending to sleep. His gut wrenched at the memory of her tears, of the way she'd lain there feigning sleep instead of confronting him. Another woman would have seized the opportunity to tell him what a bastard he was for walking out, tried to convince him to stay. Michelle was too proud for that, he realized now. She would never hold anyone against his will, never fence him in.

She was more subtle. She would make it so damn good for a man that he *couldn't* stay away.

Damn woman! What did she think she was doing? She had no right to step into his life after fifteen years and turn it upside down and mess up his plans. She had no right to make him fall head over heels in love with her again.

"I'm leaving for the day," he said, rounding his

desk, "and I don't want nobody to come looking for me." Gator slammed out the door a moment later, leaving the deputies grinning at their desks.

He drove for close to an hour, measuring the town's progress as he went. He'd busted his back over the past week, once again putting off his resignation when he saw how much there was still left to be done. It made him feel good in a way to know he had a hand in the recovery.

Gator pulled up beside the brick building that used to house the pool hall on the outskirts of town. Pitiful-looking building, he thought. Nobody had ever tried take care of it. The back door was torn completely off its hinges, a result of the storm, no doubt.

Gator stepped inside and squinted against the darkness. It was a big room, but about as shabby as they came. Heaven only knew when it had seen its last coat of paint. The pool tables were worthless, revealing rotting wood where they'd been stripped of their stained green felt. Somebody oughtta do something about this place, he thought.

"What'cha doin' here, Sheriff?"

Gator almost jumped out of his skin at the sound of the voice. He turned quickly on his heels and saw someone sitting in the shadows. There was movement, and a second later, a young boy stepped into the light streaming in from a broken window. Gator recognized the boy who'd come into his office a week ago, Billy Wilcox.

He sighed his relief. "You sneak up on me like

that again, and I'll knock you on the head with my flashlight," he said.

The boy smirked. "Aw, you ain't so tough, Sheriff. Not as tough as my old man. He could whip your butt in a heartbeat."

Gator studied the young face before him. "Is that how you got that black eye? From your daddy?" When the boy didn't answer, he went on. "Is that why you're hiding out here with the roaches?"

The boy looked partly embarrassed, partly scared. "Naw, I fell."

"Sure you did." Gator paused and looked around the room, then returned his attention to the boy. "I think I know your daddy. He hangs out at the Night Life Lounge. Drinks a little, doesn't he?"

The boy gave a hoot of a laugh. "My old man ain't never drank a little of nothin' in his whole life." His look sobered. "He don't like a damn thing I do. He says I ain't worth killin'." He touched the bruise lightly and winced. "Sometimes I think he'd like to do it personally."

"Yeah, well, that happens sometimes between fathers and sons. That doesn't mean you're bad. It just means your daddy doesn't know how to give you what you need. I think you're a pretty neat kid myself, and I don't particularly like kids, so that's quite a compliment."

"Why should I give a flip if you like me?"

Gator suppressed a smile. The kid was tough for his age. " 'Cause you and I got a lot in common, and 'cause I can get your old man off your back. If I feel like it," he added.

"What do I got to do in return?"

Gator crossed his arms over his chest and rocked back and forth on his heels. "Several things," he said. "You could check on my mother for me while I'm out of town. See that she has what she needs. And when I get back, you can be in charge of fixing up this dump." A look of incredulity passed over the boy's face. "I'll work on getting the money for it in the meantime."

The boy didn't speak for a minute. In fact, he looked about ready to cry. "You can really get my old man off my back? How?"

Gator grinned. "I have ways. Is it a deal?" He held out his hand. He wondered for a moment if the boy would take it. When he didn't make a move to do so, Gator shrugged and started to pull it back. Without warning, the boy grasped his hand tightly and pumped it with more enthusiasm than Gator was prepared for.

"All right, Sheriff!" he said. "You got yourself a deal. Just tell me where your mother lives, and I'll be out there first thing tomorrow."

And then Gator knew the boy had not been responsible for hurting his mother, and that he'd probably told the truth about the real perpetrator leaving town. Gator had accomplished more than he'd expected.

Gator's business at the Night Life Lounge took less than five minutes. He called Billy Wilcox's father outside and shoved him hard against his truck. The man, obviously drunk, covered his face out of fear.

"What's wrong with you, Wilcox? You scared to fight a man?" Gator ground out through tightly clenched lips. He knew a moment of rage that shook him to the core. He had to stay cool. He released the man, who fell to the ground.

"I ain't done nothing'!" Wilcox cried. "Why're you picking on me?"

" 'Cause I don't like grown men beating up little boys, that's why." Gator reached for the man and dragged him to his feel by his shirt collar. The man flinched when Gator pulled him close. "I'm only going to give you one warning," he said. "You lay another hand on that boy, and I'll see that you rot in jail. You hear me?"

"But Sheriff—" The man was whining now.

"And another thing. I'm going to be watching you, Wilcox. I better not catch you behind the wheel of your truck while you're all tanked up. You got that?" Gator released him with such force, he sent the man sprawling to the ground. "I suggest you find yourself a job and get off the booze, old man, 'cause I'm not going to stop riding you till you do." Gator didn't wait for him to respond. He stalked over to his truck, got in, and drove away.

On Saturday morning Michelle awoke to the sound of steady knocking. Someone was at her door. She groaned and climbed out of her bed, then padded barefoot to the living room. She threw open the door and found herself face to face with Gator Landry. For a moment she was stunned into speechlessness.

"Damn, Mic, don't you even bother to find out who's on the other side of your door before you just open it?" he asked, stepping over the threshold. He kicked the door closed behind him. "Have you any idea how many women are raped and robbed and Lord only knows what else from doing just what you did?" He didn't wait for an answer. "How can you expect law enforcement to protect you when you open your door to anyone?"

She blinked, still half-asleep. "Gator, what are you doing here? I know you didn't drive all the way up just to give me a lecture on home safety. Did you bring my car back?"

"Your car's still sitting in line at the body shop. I told you they don't hurry things along in Lizard Thicket. Mind if I sit down?" He took a seat on the couch without waiting for permission. For a moment, all he could do was stare at her in her pink shorty pajamas that brought out the flush in her cheeks. Her hair was tousled about her face beguilingly, her eyes dreamy and sleep-filled. Her long legs enticed him.

"I tired to call you at least a dozen times over the past week, Mic, but you weren't home." It had been more than a dozen, but he wasn't about to fess up and lose bargaining power. He'd practiced his speech on the drive up, but now he felt unsure.

"I've been busy."

"Oh? You been pulling double shifts at the hospital?"

"No."

So she was going to play hardball, he thought. Make him work for his information. "Does this mean you're not going to tell me what you've been up to?"

Michelle planted her hands on her hips. Oh, the nerve of the man! Here he was questioning her, after he'd walked out on her. "I told you once, Gator Landry," she began hotly, "that I don't sit home and wait for any man."

He couldn't help but grin at her show of temper. Damn, but she was cute. And sexy. And everything he'd ever wanted in a woman. Why had he ever thought he needed anything more? "Not even for me, Mic?"

"Not even for you," she said firmly.

He rose slowly from the sofa and closed the distance between them. He stopped only inches from her, leveling his gaze at her green eyes. "I've been sitting home nights over you, love."

Michelle almost shivered at his husky tone. His voice caressed her, the heat in his eyes warmed her belly. "You don't really expect me to believe that, do you? What happened, did the Night Life Lounge burn to the ground after I left?"

He chuckled and reached for her, but she took a step back. "I owe you an apology," he said.

"Damn right you do."

"I'm sorry."

She was taken off guard by the earnest look in his eyes. "You should be."

"I was scared, Mic. Terrified, in fact." He held out his hands as if surrendering. "I had to get away and clear my mind."

She felt herself softening, against her will. "What on earth could you be afraid of, Gator Landry?"

"Of falling in love with you, darlin'," he said simply. "But it's too late now, 'cause it happened, and there's not a blasted thing I can do about it. And now I realize I don't want to do anything about it. I just want to keep on lovin' you."

Her knees felt about as sturdy as warm jelly. "What about all those grand plans you had of traveling all over the world? What about those investments you were speaking of?"

Gator shot her an amused look. "You're going to make me grovel over this, aren't you?" When she didn't answer, he went on. "Remember when I told you I never felt as though I belonged?" She nodded. "That's before I realized I belonged with you. Where I go or what I do really doesn't matter anymore, as long as you're beside me."

"Maybe now, but what about next week?"

His look sobered. "I don't make decisions lightly, Mic. I wouldn't have come here if I hadn't thought this over very carefully. Hell, that's all I been doing the past week." When she continued to look doubtful, he went on. "You're the only person who ever loved me for who I am. Besides my mother," he added with a chuckle, "but that's her job. And I know you love me, Mic." He smiled tenderly, his black eyes warm. "Before you came along I felt I was not worthy of love. I thought I was a nobody, and I was scared you'd find out just how much of a nobody I was if I let you get too close."

"Oh, Gator." She felt her heart swell with love for the man, knowing how hard it was for him to tell her such things about himself.

"I've never had a high opinion of myself. It's not

important why, but I never felt I measured up. That's the real reason I didn't want to be sheriff. I was flattered when they asked me, but I was afraid I'd let them down. I was afraid I couldn't be the man my daddy was. Now I realize I only have to be myself." He shrugged and gave her a lopsided grin. "I figure if you love me, I can't be too awful bad."

Michelle was clearly touched by the confession. "Does that mean you're going to keep the job?"

"I start law enforcement training on Monday."

She shook her head, stunned at the announcement. "I'm very proud of you, Gator."

He wondered if she had any idea what those simple words meant to him. "I want you beside me, Mic," he said gently. "I'm here to offer you a job and a marriage proposal."

Michelle was clearly taken aback by his words. "You are?"

Gator still felt unsure about himself. "Perhaps you'd like to discuss the job first. It's working with a youth group I'm putting together as soon as I can squeeze the money out of those tightwads in City Hall."

She waved the statement aside. "I think I'd like to hear about the marriage proposal first, if you don't mind."

He smiled, almost shyly. "I'd like for you to be my wife, Mic," he said, and held his breath waiting for her answer. "I'll understand if you need to think about it." She continued to look at him in utter stupefaction, so he continued. "I don't care where we live as long as you'll agree to spend weekends on the houseboat with me. But you can have your house and flower beds and all that stuff women go for. I love you, Michelle. With all my heart," he added solemnly.

All at once Michelle was in his arms, laughter bubbling from her throat. Gator grinned, then captured her laughter with his lips. "Does this mean yes?" he asked when he raised his head.

"Yes!" she squealed, delighted.

"And you'll wait for me while I'm in training?" Before she could answer, he added, "I'll be able to see you weekends, and it's only for six weeks. It'll give you time to decide if you're interested in working with these kids or doing something with the hospital near Lizard Thicket." He shrugged. "Or maybe you just want to lie around naked on my houseboat for a while and make babies. We have a lot of time to make up for, love."

She nodded, unable to take her eyes off his face. He looked as radiant as any man could be. "Fifteen years' worth," she said. "I can't wait to get started."

He kissed her tenderly, fitting himself against the soft curves of her body. "The next fifteen years are going to be the happiest of your life, Mic. I'm going to be a good husband."

"I know that, Gator. You're already a good man, you know."

"Don't ever stop telling me that, darlin'. And don't ever stop telling me how much you love me and need me. I don't think I'll ever get tired of hearing it." He kissed her again. And again, until their breaths were hot and raspy. Their groans of pleasure rose over their heads.

Michelle broke the kiss. "Shouldn't we tell your mother and my grandmother?"

He pondered her question. "Maybe we should wait and tell them in person. They weren't expecting it. I don't think they even suspected we were attracted to one another."

"It'll be a shock, I'm sure."

He nodded. "We'll break it to them gently, try to get them used to the idea."

Michelle anchored her hands around his neck. "You'd think they'd have seen it coming, huh?"

Gator grinned and swooped her up in his arms with very little trouble. "We've got time to tell them. But right now we're going to concentrate on making up for lost time. Maybe if we work hard . . ."

Michelle snuggled against him as he carried her into the bedroom.

THE EDITOR'S CORNER

What could be more romantic—Valentine's Day and six LOVESWEPT romances all in one glorious month. And I have the great pleasure of writing my first editor's corner. Let me introduce myself: My name is Nita Taublib, and I have worked as an editorial consultant with the Loveswept staff since Loveswept began. As Carolyn is on vacation and Susann is still at home with her darling baby daughter, I have the honor of introducing the fabulous reading treasures we have in store for you. February is a super month for LOVESWEPT!

Deborah Smith's heroes are always fascinating, and in **THE SILVER FOX AND THE RED-HOT DOVE**, LOVESWEPT #450, the mysterious T. S. Audubon is no exception. He is intrigued by the shy Russian woman who accompanies a famous scientist to a party. And he finds himself filled with a desire to help her escape from her keepers! But when Elena Petrovic makes her own desperate escape, she is too terrified to trust him. Could her handsome enigmatic white-haired rescuer be the silver fox of her childhood fantasy, the only man who could set her loose from a hideous captivity, or does he plan to keep her for himself? Mystery and romance are combined in this passionate tale that will move you to tears.

What man could resist having a gorgeous woman as a bodyguard? Well, as Gail Douglas shows in **BANNED IN BOSTON**, LOVESWEPT #451, rugged and powerful Matt Harper never expects a woman to show up when his mother hires a security consultant to protect him after he receives a series of threatening letters. Annie Brentwood is determined to prove that the best protection de-

(continued)

mands brains, not brawn. But she forgets that she must also protect herself from the shameless, arrogant, and oh-so-male Matt, who finds himself intoxicated and intrigued by her feisty spirit. Annie finds it hard to resist a man who promises her the last word and I guarantee you will find this a hard book to put down.

Patt Bucheister's hero in **TROPICAL STORM**, LOVESWEPT #452, will make your temperature rise to sultry heights as he tries to woo Cass Mason. Wyatt Brodie has vowed to take Cass back to Key West for a reconciliation with her desperately ill mother. He challenges her to face her past, promising to help if she'll let him. Can she dare surrender to the hunger he has ignited in her yearning heart? Wyatt has warned her that once he makes love to her, they can never be just friends, that he'll fight to keep her from leaving the island. Can he claim the woman he's branded with the fire of his need? Don't miss this very touching, very emotional story.

From the sunny, sultry South we move to snowy Denver in **FROM THIS DAY FORWARD**, LOVESWEPT #453, by Joan Elliot Pickart. John-Trevor Payton has been assigned to befriend Paisley Kane to discover if sudden wealth and a reunion with the father she's never known will bring her happiness or despair. When Paisley knocks John-Trevor into a snowdrift and falls into his arms, his once firmly frozen plans for eternal bachelorhood begin to melt. Paisley has surrounded herself with a patchwork family of nutty boarders in her Denver house, and John-Trevor envies the pleasure she gets from the people she cares for. But Paisley fears she must choose between a fortune and the man destined to

(continued)

be hers. Don't miss this wonderful romance—a real treat for the senses!

Helen Mittermeyer weaves another fascinating story of two lovers reunited in **THE MASK,** LOVE-SWEPT #455. When Cas Griffith lost his young bride to a plane crash over Nepal he was full of grief and guilt and anger. He believed he'd never again want a woman as he'd desired Margo, but when he comes face-to-face with the exotic, myste-rious T'ang Qi in front of a New York art gallery two years later, he feels his body come to life again—and knows he must possess the artist who seems such an unusual combination of East and West. The reborn love discovered through their suddenly intimate embraces stuns them both as they seek to exorcise the ghosts of past heartbreak with a love that knows the true meaning of forever.

Sandra Chastain's stories fairly sizzle with pow-erful emotion and true love, and for this reason we are thrilled to bring you **DANNY'S GIRL,** LOVE-SWEPT #454. Katherine Sinclair had found it hard to resist the seductive claim Danny Dark's words had made on her heart when she was seventeen. Danny had promised to meet her after graduation, but he never came, leaving her to face a pregnancy alone. She'd given the baby up for adoption, gone to college, ended up mayor of Dark River, and never heard from Danny again . . . until now. Has he somehow discovered that she was raising her son, Mike—their son—now that his adoptive par-ents had died? Has he returned merely to try to take Mike from her? Danny still makes her burn and ache with a sizzling passion, but once they know the truth about the past, they have to dis-cover if it is love or only memory that has lasted.
(continued)

Katherine longs to show him that they are a family, that the only time she'll ever be happy is in his arms. You won't soon forget this story of two people and their son trying to become a family.

I hope that you enjoy each and every one of these Valentine treats. We've got a great year of reading pleasure in store for you. . . .

Sincerely,

Nita Taublib

Nita Taublib,
Editorial Consultant,
LOVESWEPT
Bantam Books
666 Fifth Avenue
New York, NY 10103

Starting in February . . .

An exciting, unprecedented mass market publishing program designed just for you . . . and the way you buy books!

Over the past few years, the popularity of genre authors has been unprecedented. Their success is no accident, because readers like you demand high levels of quality from your authors and reward them with fierce loyalty.

Now Bantam Books, the foremost English language mass market publisher in the world, takes another giant step in leadership by dedicating the majority of its paperback list to six genre imprints each and every month.

The six imprints that you will see wherever books are sold are:

SPECTRA.

For five years the premier publisher of science fiction and fantasy. Now Spectra expands to add one title to its list each month, a horror novel.

CRIME LINE.

The award-winning imprint of crime and mystery fiction. Crime Line will expand to embrace even more areas of contemporary suspense.

DOMAIN.

An imprint that consolidates Bantam's dominance in the frontier fiction, historical saga, and traditional Western markets.

FALCON.

High-tech action, suspense, espionage, and adventure novels will all be found in the Falcon imprint, along with Bantam's successful Air & Space and War books.

BANTAM NONFICTION.

A wide variety of commercial nonfiction, including true crime, health and nutrition, sports, reference books . . . and much more

AND NOW IT IS OUR SPECIAL PLEASURE TO INTRODUCE TO YOU THE SIXTH IMPRINT

FANFARE

FANFARE is the showcase for Bantam's popular women's fiction. With spectacular covers and even more spectacular stories. FANFARE presents three novels each month—ranging from historical to contemporary—all with great human emotion, all with great love stories at their heart, all by the finest authors writing in any genre.

FANFARE LAUNCHES IN FEBRUARY (on sale in early January) WITH THREE BREATHTAKING NOVELS . . .

THE WIND DANCER
by Iris Johansen

TEXAS! LUCKY
by Sandra Brown

WAITING WIVES
by Christina Harland

THE WIND DANCER.

From the spellbinding pen of Iris Johansen comes her most lush, dramatic, and emotionally touching romance yet—a magnificent historical about characters whose lives have been touched by the legendary Wind Dancer. A glorious antiquity, the Wind Dancer is a statue of a Pegasus that is encrusted with jewels . . . but whose worth is beyond the value of its precious stones, gold, and artistry. The Wind Dancer's origins are shrouded in the mist of time . . . and only a chosen few can unleash its mysterious powers. But WIND DANCER is, first and foremost, a magnificent love story. Set in Renaissance Italy where intrigues were as intricate as carved cathedral doors and affairs of state were ruled by affairs of the bedchamber. WIND DANCER tells the captivating story of the lovely and indomitable slave Sanchia and the man who bought her on a back street in Florence. Passionate, powerful *condottiere* Lionello Andreas would love Sanchia and endanger her with equal wild abandon as he sought to win back the prized possession of his family, the Wind Dancer.

TEXAS! LUCKY.

Turning her formidable talent for the first time to the creation of a trilogy, Sandra Brown gives readers a family to remember in the Tylers—brothers Lucky and Chase and their "little" sister Sage. In oil-bust country where Texas millionaires are becoming Texas panhandlers, the Tylers are struggling to keep their drilling business from bankruptcy. Each of the TEXAS! novels tells the love story of one member of the family and combines gritty and colorful characters with the fluid and sensual style the author is lauded for!

WAITING WIVES.

By marvelously talented newcomer Christina Harland, WAITING WIVES is the riveting tale of three vastly different women from different countries whose only bond is the fate of their men who are missing in Vietnam. In this unique novel of great human emotion, full of danger, bravery, and romance, Christina Harland brings to the written page what CHINA BEACH and TOUR OF DUTY have brought to television screens. This is a novel of triumph and honor and hope . . . and love.

Rave reviews are pouring in from critics and much-loved authors on FANFARE's novels for February—and for those in months to come. You'll be delighted and enthralled by works by Amanda Quick and Beverly Byrne, Roseanne Bittner and Kay Hooper, Susan Johnson and Nora Roberts . . . to mention only a few of the remarkable authors in the FANFARE imprint.

Special authors. Special covers. And very special stories.

Can you hear the flourish of trumpets now . . . the flourish of trumpets announcing that something special is coming?

FANFARE

Brief excerpts of the launch novels along with praise for them is on the following pages.

New York *Times* bestselling authors Catherine Coulter and Julie Garwood praise the advance copy they read of **WIND DANCER:**

"Iris Johansen is a bestselling author for the best of reasons—she's a wonderful storyteller. Sanchia, Lion, Lorenzo, and Caterina will wrap themselves around your heart and move right in. Enjoy, I did!"
—Catherine Coulter

"So compelling, so unforgettable a page-turner, this enthralling tale could have been written only by Iris Johansen. I never wanted to leave the world she created with Sanchia and Lion at its center."
—Julie Garwood

In the following brief excerpt you'll see why *Romantic Times* said this about Iris Johansen and **THE WIND DANCER:**

"The formidable talent of Iris Johansen blazes into incandescent brilliance in this highly original, mesmerizing love story."

We join the story as the evil Carpino, who runs a ring of prostitutes and thieves in Florence, is forcing the young heroine Sanchia to "audition" as a thief for the great *condottiere* Lionello, who waits in the piazza with his friend, Lorenzo, observing at a short distance.

"You're late!" Caprino jerked Sanchia into the shadows of the arcade surrounding the piazza.

"It couldn't be helped," Sanchia said breathlessly. "There was an accident . . . and we didn't get finished until the hour tolled . . . and then I had to wait until Giovanni left to take the—"

Caprino silenced the flow of words with an impatient motion of his hand. "There he is." He nodded across the crowded piazza. "The big man in the wine-colored velvet cape listening to the storyteller."

Sanchia's gaze followed Caprino's to the man standing in front of the platform. He was more than big, he was a giant, she thought gloomily. The careless arrogance in the man's stance bespoke perfect confidence in his ability to deal with any circumstances and, if he caught her, he'd probably use his big strong hands to crush her head like a walnut. Well, she was too tired to worry about that now. It had been over thirty hours since she had slept. Perhaps it was just as well she was almost too exhausted to care what happened to her. Fear must not make her as clumsy as she had been yesterday. She was at least glad the giant appeared able to afford to lose a few ducats. The richness of his clothing indicated he must either be a great lord or a prosperous merchant.

"Go." Caprino gave her a little push out onto the piazza. "Now."

She pulled her shawl over her head to shadow her face and hurried toward the platform where a man was telling a story, accompanying himself on the lyre.

A drop of rain struck her face, and she glanced up at the suddenly dark skies. Not yet, she thought with exasperation. If it started to rain in earnest the people crowding the piazza would run for shelter and she would have to follow the velvet-clad giant until he put himself into a situation that allowed her to make the snatch.

Another drop splashed her hand, and her anxious gaze flew to the giant. His attention was still fixed on the storyteller, but only the saints knew how long he would remain engrossed. This storyteller was not very good. Her pace quickened as she flowed like a shadow into the crowd surrounding the platform.

Garlic, Lion thought, as the odor assaulted his nostrils. Garlic, spoiled fish, and some other stench that smelled even fouler. He glanced around the crowd trying to identify the source of the smell. The people surrounding the platform were the same ones he had studied moments before, trying to search out Caprino's thief. The only new arrival was a thin woman dressed in a shabby gray gown, an equally ragged woolen shawl covering her head.

She moved away from the edge of the crowd and started to hurry across the piazza. The stench faded with her departure and Lion drew a deep breath. *Dio*, luck was with him in this, at least. He was not at all pleased at being forced to stand in the rain waiting for Caprino to produce his master thief.

"It's done," Lorenzo muttered, suddenly at Lion's side. He had been watching from the far side of the crowd. Now he said more loudly, "As sweet a snatch as I've ever seen."

"What?" Frowning, Lion gazed at him. "There was no—" He broke off as he glanced down at his belt. The pouch was gone; only the severed cords remained in his belt. "Sweet Jesus." His gaze flew around the piazza. "Who?"

"The sweet madonna who looked like a beggar maid and smelled like a decaying corpse." Lorenzo nodded toward the arched arcade. "She disappeared behind that column, and I'll wager you'll find Caprino lurking there with her, counting your ducats."

Lion started toward the column. "A woman," he murmured. "I didn't expect a woman. How good is she?"

Lorenzo fell into step with him. "Very good."

Iris Johansen's fabulous romances of characters whose lives are touched by the Wind Dancer go on! STORM WINDS, coming from FANFARE in June 1991, is another historical. REAP THE WIND, a contemporary, will be published by FANFARE in November 1991.

Sandra Brown, whose legion of fans catapulted her last contemporary novel onto the *New York Times* list, has received the highest praise in advance reviews of **TEXAS! LUCKY.** *Rave Reviews* said, "Romance fans will relish all of Ms. Brown's provocative sensuality along with a fast-paced plotline that springs one surprise after another. Another feast for the senses from one of the world's hottest pens."

Indeed Sandra's pen is "hot"—especially so in her incredible **TEXAS!** trilogy. We're going to peek in on an early episode in which Lucky has been hurt in a brawl in a bar where he was warding off the attentions of two town bullies toward a redhead he hadn't met, but wanted to get to know very well.

This woman was going to be an exciting challenge, something rare that didn't come along every day. Hell, he'd never had anybody exactly like her.

"What's your name?"

She raised deep forest-green eyes to his. "D-D Dovey."

" 'D-D Dovey'?"

"That's right," she snapped defensively. "What's wrong with it?"

"Nothing. I just hadn't noticed your stuttering before. Or has the sight of my bare chest made you develop a speech impediment?"

"Hardly. Mr.—?"

"Lucky."

"Mr. Lucky?"

"No, I'm Lucky."

"Why is that?"

"I mean my name is Lucky. Lucky Tyler."

"Oh. Well. I assure you the sight of your bare chest leaves me cold, Mr. Tyler."

He didn't believe her and the smile that tilted up one corner of his mouth said so. "Call me Lucky."

She reached for the bottle of whiskey on the nightstand and raised it in salute. "Well, Lucky, your luck just ran out."

"Huh?"

"Hold your breath." Before he could draw a sufficient one, she tipped the bottle and drizzled the liquor over the cut.

He blasted the four walls with words unfit to be spoken aloud, much less shouted. "Oh hell, oh—"

"Your language isn't becoming to a gentleman, Mr. Tyler."

"I'm gonna murder you. Stop pouring that stuff— Agh!"

"You're acting like a big baby."

"What the hell are you trying to do, scald me?"

"Kill the germs."

"Damn! It's killing *me*. Do something. Blow on it."

"That only causes germs to spread."

"Blow on it!"

She bent her head over his middle and blew gently along the cut. Her breath fanned his skin and cooled the stinging whiskey in the open wound. Droplets of it had collected in the satiny stripe of hair beneath his navel. Rivulets trickled beneath the waistband of his jeans. She blotted at them with her fingertips, then, without thinking, licked the liquor off her own skin. When she realized what she'd done, she sprang upright. "Better now?" she asked huskily.

When Lucky's blue eyes connected with hers, it was like completing an electric circuit. The atmosphere crackled. Matching her husky tone of voice, he said, "Yeah, much better. . . . Thanks," he mumbled. Her hand felt so comforting and cool, the way his mother's always had whenever he was sick with fever. He captured Dovey's hand with his and pressed it against his hot cheek.

She withdrew it and, in a schoolmarm's voice, said, "You can stay only until the swelling goes down."

"I don't think I'll be going anywhere a-tall tonight," he said. "I feel like hell. This is all I want to do. Lie here. Real still and quiet."

Through a mist of pain, he watched her remove her jacket and drape it over the back of a chair. Just as he'd thought—quite a looker was Dovey. But that wasn't all. She looked like a woman who knew her own mind and wasn't afraid to speak it. Levelheaded.

So what the hell had she been doing in that bar? He drifted off while puzzling through the question.

Now on sale in DOUBLEDAY hardcover is the next in Sandra's fantastic trilogy, TEXAS! CHASE, about which *Rendezvous* has said: ". . . it's the story of a love that is deeper than the oceans, and more lasting than the land itself. Lucky's story was fantastic; Chase's story is more so." FANFARE's paperback of TEXAS! CHASE will go on sale August 1991.

Rather than excerpt from the extraordinary novel **WAITING WIVES,** which focuses on three magnificent women, we will describe the book in some detail. The three heroines whom you'll love and root for give added definition to the words growth and courage . . . and love.

ABBRA is talented and sheltered, a raven-haired beauty who was just eighteen when she fell rapturously in love with handsome Army captain Lewis Ellis. Immediately after their marriage he leaves for Vietnam. Passionately devoted to Lewis, she lives for his return—until she's told he's dead. Then her despair turns to torment as she falls hopelessly in love with Lewis's irresistible brother. . . .

SERENA never regrets her wildly impulsive marriage to seductive Kyle Anderson. But she does regret her life of unabashed decadence and uninhibited pleasure—especially when she discovers a dirty, bug-infested orphanage in Saigon . . . and Kyle's illegitimate child.

GABRIELLE is the daughter of a French father and a Vietnamese mother. A flame-haired singer with urchin appeal and a sultry voice, she is destined for stardom. But she gives her heart—and a great part of her future—to a handsome Aussie war correspondent. Gavin is determined to record the "real" events of the Vietnam war . . . but his search for truth leads him straight into the hands of the Viet Cong and North Vietnamese, who have no intention of letting him report anything until they've won the war.

Christina Harland is an author we believe in. Her story is one that made all of us who work on FANFARE cry, laugh, and turn pages like mad. We predict that WAITING WIVES will fascinate and enthrall you . . . and that you will say with us, "it is a novel whose time has come."

We hope you will greet FANFARE next month with jubilation! It is an imprint we believe you will delight in month after month, year after year to come.

THE
"VIVE LA ROMANCE"
SWEEPSTAKES

Don't miss your chance to speak to your favorite Loveswept authors on the LOVESWEPT LINE 1-900-896-2505*

You may win a glorious week for two in the world's most romantic city, Paris, France by entering the "Vive La Romance" sweepstakes when you call. With travel arrangements made by Reliable Travel, you and that special someone will fly American Airlines to Paris, where you'll be guests at the famous Lancaster Hotel. Why not call right now? Your own Loveswept fantasy could come true!

Official Rules:

1. **No Purchase Is Necessary**. Enter by calling 1-900-896-2505 and following the directions for entry. The phone call will cost $.95 per minute and the average time necessary to enter the sweepstakes will be two minutes or less with either a touch tone or a rotary phone, when you choose to enter at the beginning of the call. Or you can enter by handprinting your name, address and telephone number on a plain 3" x 5" card and sending it to:

> **VIVE LA ROMANCE SWEEPSTAKES**
> **Department CK**
> **BANTAM BOOKS**
> **666 Fifth Avenue**
> **New York, New York 10103**

Copies of the Official Rules can be obtained by sending a request along with a self-addressed stamped envelope to: Vive La Romance Sweepstakes, Bantam Books, Department CK-2, 666 Fifth Avenue, New York, New York 10103. Residents of Washington and Vermont need not include return postage. Requests must be received by November 30, 1990.

*Callers must be 18 or older. Each call costs 95¢ per minute. See official rules for details.

Official Rules cont'd

2. 1 Grand Prize: A vacation trip for two to Paris, France for 7 nights. Trip includes accommodations at the deluxe Lancaster Hotel and round-trip coach tickets to Paris on American Airlines from the American Airlines airport nearest the winner's residence which provides direct service to New York.
(Approximate Retail Value: $3,500).

3. Sweepstakes begins October 1, 1990 and all entries must be received by December 31, 1990. All entrants must be 18 years of age or older at the time of entry. The winner will be chosen by Bantam's Marketing Department by a random drawing to be held on or about January 15, 1991 from all entries received and will be notified by mail. Bantam's decision is final. The winner has 30 days from date of notice in which to accept the prize award or an alternate winner will be chosen. The prize is not transferable and no substitution is allowed. The trip must be taken by November 22, 1991, and is subject to airline departure schedules and ticket and accommodation availability. Certain blackout periods may apply. Winner must have a valid passport. Odds of winning depend on the number of entries received. Enter as often as you wish, but each mail-in entry must be entered separately. No mechanically reproduced entries allowed.

4. The winner and his or her guest will be required to execute an Affidavit of Eligibility and Promotional Release supplied by Bantam. Entering the sweepstakes constitutes permission for use of winner's name, address and likeness for publicity and promotional purposes, with no additional compensation or permission.

5. This sweepstakes is open only to residents of the U.S. who are 18 years of age or older, and is void in Puerto Rico and wherever else prohibited or restricted by law. Employees of Bantam Books, Bantam Doubleday Dell Publishing Group, Inc., Reliable Travel, Call Interactive, their subsidiaries and affiliates, and their immediate family members are not eligible to enter this sweepstakes. Taxes, if any, are the winner's sole responsibility.

6. Bantam is the sole sponsor of the sweepstakes. Bantam reserves the right to cancel the sweepstakes via the 900 number at any time and without prior notice, but entry into the sweepstakes via mail through December 31, 1990 will remain. Bantam is not responsible for lost, delayed or misdirected entries, and Bantam, Call Interactive, and AT&T are not responsible for any error, incorrect or inaccurate entry of information by entrants, malfunctions of the telephone network, computer equipment software or any combination thereof. This Sweepstakes is subject to the complete Official Rules.

7. For the name of the prize winner (available after January 15, 1991), send a stamped, self-addressed envelope entirely separate from your entry to:

VIVE LA ROMANCE SWEEPSTAKES WINNER LIST,
Bantam Books, Dept. CK-3, 666 Fifth Avenue,
New York, New York 10103.

Loveswept ®